The Rivenhall Weddings

A brand-new trilogy from Carol Arens

The three children of Viscount Rivenhall couldn't be more different: serious Thomas feels the responsibility of his position as heir, while fun-loving William struggles to settle down. But even he hasn't the same capacity for causing scandal as his younger sister, Minerva!

Now it is time for all three to be wed— but will they marry as they are expected to?

William's story:
Inherited as the Gentleman's Bride

Thomas's story:
In Search of a Viscountess

Available now

And look out for Minerva's story, coming soon!

Author Note

I hope this letter finds you well and you have an abundance of books to read this summer. There's nothing quite like the company of a good story to take us to a place long ago and far away.

Thank you so much for picking up a copy of *In Search of a Viscountess*. If you read the first book in The Rivenhall Weddings series, *Inherited as the Gentleman's Bride*, you will have met Thomas Grant. There could not be a more serious fellow or one more dedicated to the pursuit of one day becoming a proper viscount. He devotes his life to behaving in a way that brings honor to the family, even going so far as to choose a lady to court who will fill a role as viscountess rather than fill a place in his heart. However, we both know that his plans will be turned upside down. Luckily, he hires a companion for his sister who does just that. Evie Clarke is a lady determined to remind him how to have fun. In the end, what she teaches him is the value of love.

I hope you enjoy Evie and Thomas's journey to their happily-ever-after.

CAROL ARENS

—

In Search of a Viscountess

ISBN-13: 978-1-335-72326-0

In Search of a Viscountess

Copyright © 2022 by Carol Arens

Recycling programs
for this product may
not exist in your area.

This is a work of fiction. Names, characters, places and incidents
are either the product of the author's imagination or are used fictitiously.
Any resemblance to actual persons, living or dead, businesses,
companies, events or locales is entirely coincidental.

For questions and comments about the quality of this book,
please contact us at CustomerService@Harlequin.com.

Harlequin Enterprises ULC
22 Adelaide St. West, 41st Floor
Toronto, Ontario M5H 4E3, Canada
www.Harlequin.com

Printed in U.S.A.

Carol Arens delights in tossing fictional characters into hot water, watching them steam and then giving them a happily-ever-after. When she is not writing, she enjoys spending time with her family, beach camping or lounging about a mountain cabin. At home, she enjoys playing with her grandchildren and gardening. During rare spare moments, you will find her snuggled up with a good book. Carol enjoys hearing from readers at carolarens@yahoo.com or on Facebook.

Books by Carol Arens

Harlequin Historical

The Cowboy's Cinderella
Western Christmas Brides
"A Kiss from the Cowboy"
The Rancher's Inconvenient Bride
A Ranch to Call Home
A Texas Christmas Reunion
The Earl's American Heiress
Rescued by the Viscount's Ring
The Making of Baron Haversmere
The Viscount's Yuletide Bride
To Wed a Wallflower
A Victorian Family Christmas
"A Kiss Under the Mistletoe"
The Viscount's Christmas Proposal

The Rivenhall Weddings

Inherited as the Gentleman's Bride
In Search of a Viscountess

Visit the Author Profile page
at Harlequin.com for more titles.

To Justin Lopez,

my much loved son-in-law,
a man of faith and many talents.

Chapter One

October 1887

Violet Evie Dumel did not believe in ghostly spirits. But if she were to begin doing so, the wee dark hours of this October night would be the time.

Quietly closing the back door of Gossmere House behind her, she stepped onto the porch, listening to the wind whooshing, watching shadows stretch and shift, playing tricks on her eyes.

It was true that her nerves were taut. Naturally they would be since she was running away. Escaping, truth be told, from a place that was no longer her beloved home.

Leaves tumbling across the ground seemed to be whispering a warning…'risky'…'perilous'.

Lifting her skirt with one hand and dashing away a tear with the other, she hurried down the steps. Leaving home felt like slicing her soul in half. However, Gossmere had not truly been home since her parents had died last year of scarlet fever and her father's cousin had come to take Father's place as Baron.

A small dark shape dashed across her path, quickly seen and then gone. It was lucky she did not believe in black cats bringing bad luck. But even if she did believe it, the cat had been a kitten so it could not really be a great deal of bad luck.

The truth was, she was running away for the purpose of making her own luck. Good luck. If she remained here, the only luck she would have would be cursed, miserable luck.

The kitten chased a leaf, then turned and dashed for the hem of her skirt. It dug its small claws into the fabric and began to climb.

'All right then.' She unhooked the clinging creature, lifted it to her cheek, enjoying the soft brush of fur on her skin. 'This is the worst timing to adopt a pet but still, I shall bring you with me—a talisman for good luck.'

Holding it at arm's length, she gazed into a face that was quite adorable. The kitten's eyes were green rather than newborn blue, so clearly it was old enough to be weaned from its mother and yet young enough that it was still fluffy and quite small.

'You shall be good luck and a reminder of home as it used to be. I will name you Charm. I hope you like it.'

Pressing Charm to her galloping heart, she hurried up the lane that led to the road. All along the way she prayed that Mary, her neighbour and dearest friend in the world, had managed to get her father's phaeton away from their stable undetected.

If Mary did not manage, Violet's future would be in peril.

'I will not marry that old man,' she told the kitten. 'I do not care how much money he offers Hubert for me.'

She had met Baron Falcon weeks ago and felt that not only was he dislikeable but he had a lecherous eye. An eye which she had felt lingering upon her in an unwholesome, completely inappropriate way.

It had been the hardest thing she had ever done not to recoil from his grip on her arm when he'd led her into dinner that night. Later, she had been forced to invent a stomach ailment to avoid walking with him in the garden. Although it had not been a great invention since her stomach had actually recoiled in nausea over the prospect.

She had given no outward sign of rebellion, not then or not any time since. It would not do for Cousin Hubert to suspect what she was up to. Let him believe she was a willing sacrifice in his quest to further his new-found wealth.

'Even if Baron Falcon was a prince I would still be running away,' she admitted to Charm. 'The choice of a husband is mine to make.'

Her wonderful parents had always made it clear that such an important decision would be hers. Yes, Father had been Baron Gossmere, a man of society, however he'd been a rare one. He'd believed that a woman ought to make her own choice—that it was her right to do so.

Cousin Hubert and his wife, Ada, were of the wrong and unenlightened belief that she was their asset to do with as they pleased. What pleased them was to offer her to Baron Falcon for a large sum of money.

'The money that comes with Gossmere is not enough for them, you understand.' Charm meowed, then licked his, or perhaps it was her, small paw while Violet hurried towards the road. 'Indeed not. They are a glum and selfish couple. You and I are well away from them. But then you are lucky to be a cat and not ruined by an unfair entail. Curse primogeniture, I say.'

But no! She would not be ruined, she refused to be.

So far there was no sign of Mary and the phaeton. That was a worry. She could hardly run away without transportation.

Stepping into the dark shadow of a tree, she watched the road, glancing now and again back at the house. The windows remained dark. Apparently, they were still unaware that she had run away. She listened hard for wheels on gravel but all she heard was wind eerily moaning through branches.

Getting the carriage out of the stable without observation was the trickiest part of this scheme. And the most important part. If Mary failed at this…well, it made her shiver.

Tomorrow, Baron Falcon would be arriving to make a proposal, believing she would accept it.

She must be away, even if she was forced to sprint. Going on foot was not a brilliant escape plan since as soon as she was missed she would be caught on the road then hauled home to face disaster.

'Oh, there! Do you hear it?' she whispered to the kitten. Relief ought to quieten her heart, but it went on pounding against her ribs. Just because she heard a carriage approaching did not mean it was the one she was waiting for. Although who else would be on the road at this time of night?

It seemed that an eternity passed before the phaeton rounded the bend in the road.

Oh, dear...oh, drat! Mary was not alone!

'I got caught,' Mary explained, motioning for Violet to hurry towards the carriage. 'Luckily it was Gregory who caught me. He has agreed to help. In thanks, I will ask Father for an increase in his stable hand's pay.'

'In any case, Miss,' Gregory said to Mary, 'I could not let you go out in the night without protection.'

'You are our prince,' Violet stated, meaning it even if his motivation was an increase in pay.

Leaping off the carriage, he gave her a hand up. Hopefully he would remain princely and not, in the end, give them away.

Glancing in the back of the carriage, she spotted a trunk. Over the past weeks Violet had been giving Mary items of her clothing to be secreted away. Even so, she had been forced to leave some of her favourite belongings behind. The important thing was, she had enough to get by.

'What have you got there?' Mary asked, reaching for the kitten.

'This is Charm. I am hoping she, or he, will bring me luck.'

Or, if not that, the kitten would be a friend in a city where she knew no one. Even though they were now on their way, she would still need luck on her side.

Mary took Charm, turned the kitten to peer at its backside then, with a smile, handed it back. 'She.'

It gave her a bit of courage, seeing her friend's grin.

There was still the matter of becoming employed to be accomplished. In a week's time she had an interview for the position of companion to a lady only a little younger than she was.

If she had any hope of making a success of living independently she would need funds. What she had would not last terribly long.

Mary passed her an envelope, her father's red wax seal securing the seam. 'Lord Haverly has no idea what a glowing letter of reference he has written on your behalf.'

'I'm sure your father was quite complimentary.'

Quite, since Mary had written said compliments.

'I will miss you, Violet.' Mary smiled, clearly putting on a show of courage. 'I wish you did not have to go.'

It was the worst part of all this, leaving Mary. Having grown up as lively as raindrops bouncing in mud puddles, sharing hopes and dreaming dreams, they were going to miss each other dreadfully.

Now, in the face of Violet's peril, Mary had proved what a grand friend she really was.

Hugging Charm close to her heart, Violet stared at the road stretching ahead and took a stranglehold on her tears.

The least she could do was behave as bravely as Mary.

With a defeated sigh, Thomas Grant watched the butler escort yet another applicant for the position of his sister's companion out of the house.

Heavy-hearted, he walked towards the small drawing room where Minerva sat on the divan, her attention focused on a red flower she was stitching. If not for the fact that Minerva hated stitching, he would be happy to see her occupied in this demure, ladylike pursuit.

Keeping his sister in line while his father, Lord Rivenhall, was on holiday in Scotland was a challenge of the highest order. And one he'd taken to heart.

As future Viscount, Thomas would need to do everything as well as his father did. The prospect was a daunting one. While his father did not own a vast country estate, he did own several properties. Learning everything about the running of them took up the better part of his time. More than ever he admired his father. Standing in his shoes, if only temporarily, was an honour.

While his father had put on a brave face and called his trip to Scotland a holiday, he had also revealed that he was ill with some lingering ailment. In Thomas's mind lingering ailments were concerning, an indication that one's body was struggling in the effort to fight off whatever was making it weak.

Although his father did not appear to be weak. Hopefully the extended rest would aid his recovery.

The Good Lord willing, Thomas would not be required to step into the role of Viscount for many more years, but it could not be discounted. He had always striven to be the son, the future heir, his father was teaching him to be. Now he was ill, and on holiday, it fell to Thomas to behave more responsibly than ever.

The best outcome would be for his father to return home restored to health and commending him for his faithful handling of all that came with acting as Lord Rivenhall.

At the worst…well, he would not dwell on the worst. He would simply perform his duty.

Of all the obligations his father had entrusted to him, keeping Minerva in line was the most challenging. If there was one thing his sister did not wish, it was to be kept in line. It was almost unnerving to see her sitting on the couch, needle in hand while she hummed. Even as a child she had been clever and opinionated. As she grew, those traits became more pronounced.

Thomas still felt sick at heart remembering the time, and not terribly long ago, when he had come out of the front door of Rivenhall to find a crowd of mostly young men watching Minerva merrily gliding through the air on a swing she had attached to the big tree. Even now he felt his face flush, remembering the skimpy costume she had worn. To this day she defended it as perfectly respectable circus attire.

In case that was not bad enough, she had compounded the scandal by hanging a banner over the front door proclaiming that she would never wed, that callers would be shunned—those were the words written by her own hand!

Staring at Minerva, so dedicated to doing something she detested, he could only wonder who she was. It was almost as if this young woman was a stranger in his sister's form.

He stood in front of her, arms folded across his chest in a stance he had seen his father use many times.

'Minerva, are you ill?' Truly, that was the only explanation for her odd behaviour.

'I cannot imagine why you would think so. Am I not behaving in a perfectly appropriate way?'

'Appropriate for someone else.'

She set the stitching project aside, cocked her head and blinked at him, her eyes wide and innocent-looking.

The hairs on the back of his neck stood to attention. His sister was not one to blink in wide-eyed innocence.

'Is this not the behaviour you seek to achieve by hiring me a governess, brother?'

'Not a governess. We both know you are past the age for it.'

He refrained from pointing out that any governess his father had ever hired regretted taking the position.

Not that his sister was in any way mean-spirited—she was simply…spirited.

'A companion would—'

'Be the same thing as a governess!' Standing suddenly, Minerva slammed her hands on her hips, narrowing her gaze upon him.

That was more like the Minerva he knew and loved—and worried greatly about.

'Many of your friends have married already. Surely you would enjoy having a companion?'

'I might, if I were not required to walk as slowly as a snail in order to match her doddering steps. The ladies you are interviewing are ancient. Perhaps you would like to join us while my companion recounts her life's experiences, regales the joys of being young in bygone days, when everything was better than it is now.'

Presented that way, it did seem tedious.

'I will accept the next applicant if you agree to sit with us while we have grand times reading.' She shot a scathing glance at her needlework. 'Or stitching.'

He should not say it but, dash it, it did bear bringing

up because it was obviously correct. 'You would not need a companion if you married.'

Without a word, she sat down, picked up her needlework and retreated into the person he did not know.

'There are some very decent gentlemen who would be happy to be courting you,' he persisted.

If he managed to get Minerva interested in a fellow by the time his father returned, it would be well received and a comfort to him if— But no, Father would surely return cured of whatever malady was troubling him.

'I would make him miserable since I have no wish to become anyone's wife. You are the one who ought to be courting, Thomas.'

She was quite correct. But that was not the point at the moment. He would not allow this conversation to be diverted to another subject.

'Look at your married friends, Minnie. Don't they seem happy?'

'Of course they do, since marriage is what they wanted. But, I promise you, had their dream been to become trapeze artists…to perform daring feats of agility and grace, they would not be happy.'

Perhaps he should send his sister to visit his brother and sister-in-law. Minerva enjoyed being with them at Wilton Farm and was quite attached to the babies.

But no, that would be transferring his responsibility to William. Thomas was the one in line to become Viscount and therefore, in Father's absence, bore the obligation of overseeing his sister's future.

It was hard to imagine that little more than a year ago William had been the rascal of the family. Thomas hated to think of all the times his brother had caused tongues to wag. Clearly, a good marriage could make a great difference in a person.

With any luck he would exact such a change in his headstrong sister. If by the time his father returned she was settled and eager…or, if not eager, at least not opposed to seeking an engagement, it would demonstrate how worthy a Viscount he would one day be.

Not that he really needed to prove himself. Ever since he was a twelve-year-old lad he had set his course on learning all he could in order to be a proper heir apparent. Perhaps he had sacrificed fun and adventure in the effort but even as a child he understood that one day he would be a man with many people depending upon him.

The word *responsible* described him rather well and he was happy with it. Sober-minded—he liked that too.

'I can see what you are thinking, Thomas.'

His sister was too skilled at reading his thoughts. William complained of the same thing.

'I do not believe you can.'

'You think that if you can convince me to court some gentleman, you will gain Father's approval. But if you want to know what I think, it is your own approval you are after.'

'That is not true. I am simply trying to hire a companion for your amusement.'

It was nearly the truth. He meant proper amusement for a young lady. He hoped a mature companion would guide Minerva away from trouble.

'If it is Father's approval you wish,' she went on as if he had not spoken, 'you should begin courting. That would please him greatly.'

She was right. He ought to have begun the process

long ago, but the time had never seemed right. Now, however, with his father's illness, he needed to take this obligation more seriously.

'Once you accept a suitable companion, perhaps I will.'

He might as well use the situation to his advantage.

'It will do no good to try and put your lack of interest in marriage on my shoulders. Whether or not I accept a companion has nothing to do with your decision and you well know it.'

'What if I do mean it? If I begin to search for a wife, will you accept suitors?'

'Suitors?' She was too sharp to miss the way he'd turned the conversation, but he did have to try. 'This is about you courting and me accepting a companion.'

'Very well,' he amended. 'You will allow me to engage an appropriate lady.'

'I doubt very much that your idea of appropriate and mine are remotely alike. However, you will seek a bride?' Laughter danced in her eyes. He had no idea if she would accept or decline.

Since he did need to seek a wife, he was not above using the occasion to get what he wanted from his sister. The opportunity might not present itself again.

'I will. What do you say, Minnie?'

He truly hoped that an experienced older woman would be just the person to guide Minerva in selecting an appropriate suitor.

'Agreed.' She held out her hand. 'We must shake on it to make it binding.'

This had worked out better than he'd expected. It was not often that he got the best of Minerva.

Footsteps tapped down the hallway then stopped in the drawing room doorway.

Thomas turned towards the sound, nodded at the butler.

'Miss Evie Clarke is here for her appointment with you, sir.'

Good, perhaps this lady would be the one.

Chapter Two

Upon stepping out of the hired cab and seeing the Rivenhall townhouse for the first time, Violet's breath rushed out of her lungs in admiration.

The house was magnificent and yet not ostentatious. Many of the homes the cab had passed in this elegant area seemed intimidating. She could not imagine living in one of them.

She did not feel that way about the house she was standing in front of—and staring agog at. Somehow, and she could not quite explain why, she felt drawn to it. All she could think was that in a small way it reminded her of home. However, quite a bit larger and more resplendent.

Gossmere was a lovely manor, perfect in every way for a country baron. But the Rivenhall house… My stars, it was certainly fit for a Viscount. Even though Violet was a respectable lady of society, she'd had a sheltered upbringing in the country. Even Mary's home was not nearly as impressive as this one.

Staring out of the cab window on the ride here, she

had been in awe of the regal homes and the number of people on the streets. Her jaw had positively dropped at the wealth of places to shop.

Her allowance, if she managed to secure the position, would probably not allow for many purchases, but she imagined the lady for whom she hoped to be a companion would be able to snatch up everything her heart took a fancy to.

She rather looked forward to such an outing.

Coming up the brick path leading to the door, a rain of golden leaves trickled down from a giant tree. They drifted about her in a lovely swirl. The air was cool and crisp. She inhaled deeply, taking in the scent of autumn. She utterly adored this time of year.

The three-storey brick house was topped by an attic with several dormers. The front of the house had so many windows she could not take the time to count them. And how charming were the window boxes? Each one fairly dripped in flowers of gold, yellow and red.

It was clear to see this home was cherished. She could easily imagine living here. All she needed to do was shine brighter than the other applicants for the companion position, who could only be more qualified than she was.

Although they were not likely to have a more glowing letter of reference. On the train ride to London she had read what 'Lord Haverly'—Mary—had written. With such glowing praise, it was likely the Queen herself would give Miss Evie Clarke a position.

Looking up at the brick house, at the windows decked in lace curtains, then down at the lovely grounds on either side of the path, she wondered if the Viscount—

or rather the Viscount's heir, as he was the one who would be interviewing her—would expect her to use the back door.

Hesitating for a half second only, she continued on her way towards the front porch, climbing the steps. She straightened her shoulders, reminding herself that she was the daughter of a Baron.

As a companion, she would be considered a family friend more than an employee. Going around the back to the servants' entrance would be inappropriate.

Within seconds of her knock, the butler opened the door.

She introduced herself as Evie Clarke. She did not dare use her actual name for fear of being found out. It was unlikely that Hubert and Ada would easily give up their scheme of using her to gain greater wealth.

With a nod, the butler bent slightly at the waist, inviting her to enter.

He led her through a foyer which was utterly elegant and at the same time welcoming. Flowers in bright hues of autumn filled vases on both sides of the hallway he led her along.

Three doors down, the butler stopped, indicating she should wait while he announced her.

She hoped he took his time about it because she spotted a lovely vase across the hall and wanted to take a closer look at the yellow lilies accented by dark green ferns. She went quickly to the arrangement then bent her nose, sniffing deeply.

Oh, how very lovely! If there was one thing she adored it was flowers. If only it was possible to make a gown of blossoms! Now that would be pure heaven.

'Miss Clarke? Mr Grant will see you now.' The butler had returned so quietly she jumped at the sound of his voice.

The starched-looking fellow's mouth twitched at one corner as she passed by him to enter the drawing room. One of his eyebrows lifted. How very odd.

A tall man who looked to be in his early thirties stood with his hands behind his back. For an instant his expression held the same puzzled expression that the butler's had.

That was strange, since she did have an appointment and so would be expected.

'Miss Clarke, welcome to Rivenhall. I am Thomas Grant and this is my sister, Minerva.'

Mr Grant smiled at her, but his expression looked strained and his dark brows lowered. The gesture nearly hid the beautiful forget-me-not shade of his eyes. She was left to wonder if, for some reason she could not understand, she was not in fact welcome.

Perhaps Mary's reference had been too glowing and he suspected it to be a forgery. Oh, please do not let that be true. She needed this position so desperately.

'It is a pleasure to meet you, Mr Grant.'

'And a pleasure to meet you, Miss Clarke.' She hoped he actually thought so. 'Won't you have a seat?' With a nod, he indicated a plush gold velvet chair and then he sat down on the one across from it.

Even though he said she was welcome, the thin press of his lips did not indicate it to be true.

The young lady, Minerva, rose from her place on the couch then took a chair nearby. She tossed aside the needlework she had been working on, not seeming to care that it slipped from the couch to the floor.

'It is rather a great pleasure to meet you, Miss Clarke,' she said. 'But please do call me Minerva.'

Violet—Evie that was, she must get used to using her middle name—thought that, being of a similar age, she and Minerva would get along well.

However, she could only wonder why the young woman was seeking a companion rather than a husband. She was pretty enough that she ought to have had a dozen proposals of marriage by now.

Of course, both Minerva and her brother were probably wondering the same thing about her. She was of an age to seek a husband, after all. Or to run from an unwanted one.

All of a sudden she became aware that Thomas Grant was again giving her that quizzical glance he had when she'd first walked into the drawing room.

For a man who seemed a less than cheerful sort, he was quite attractive. It was usually easy-natured gentlemen who caught her eye. A quick genuine smile had the power to turn the plainest face handsome.

Mr Grant did not have a plain face, though. In fact, he was handsome, compellingly so. Not even that strained smile could hide it.

Her stomach felt like a net of madly flapping butterflies, and not because of his good looks. Rather, it was because she had the worst feeling that she was failing this interview before she'd even had a chance to present a case for the brilliant companion she would be to Minerva.

The young lady she would be companion to seemed

willing to have her, but her brother, who would be the one to decide, did not.

Her hopes of getting this position were beginning to dim rather quickly.

Oh, my stars, what was she to do if she did not get it? Perhaps she should not have, but she had pinned her hopes and her future on this.

Thomas was stunned at his first glimpse of the new applicant.

Flummoxed and confused.

Miss Clarke was not at all like the other ladies he had interviewed today. She was young, very pretty with a bright friendly smile. Her eyes held what he thought were equal parts anticipation and nervousness.

What, he wondered rather sceptically, was she doing seeking a position when she ought to be seeking a husband? Ladies hoping to become a companion had typically fallen on hard times, widowhood or some other loss of income.

While being young and pretty did not exclude hard circumstances or widowhood, her letter of reference did not indicate either to be the case. And she did go by the title Miss.

An older, experienced lady was what he had in mind to keep Minerva grounded. He had concerns about the suitability of someone so young...and about someone who had a bright orange spot on the tip of her nose. Pollen, he imagined, from taking a sniff of the lilies in the hallway.

In reading her letter of reference, a letter from a gentleman he was acquainted with and knew to be reliable, she was an experienced and capable candidate for the position.

To him, it did not seem likely that at her age she had so much experience. Perhaps she was capable, though.

And yet it worried him that she was not wed. Was it by choice or circumstance? Ordinarily, it would be none of his business. But in this instance it was important to know. If the reason was that she did not believe in marriage, she would not be the right companion for Minerva. He needed a lady who would encourage his sister to think of marriage in a positive light.

Miss Clarke was a hard one to judge by simply looking at her. She was dressed neatly and fashionably, which spoke well of her. Her lips presented a demure, modest smile. But her eyes troubled him. They twinkled in a way suspiciously like his sister's eyes did.

What if Miss Clarke and Minerva were peas in a pod, so to speak?

The thought made him tremble.

Miss Evie Clarke wore her hair in a tidy bun tied at the nape of her neck. He found himself captivated by springy little curls that popped out here and there, framing her pretty round face and the graceful turn of her neck.

He ought to slap himself for wanting to pull a curl straight to see it bounce merrily back into place. This was an interview for a companion for his sister, not for himself.

According to the reference letter, Evie Clarke was the daughter of one Baron Brisby. In this she was an acceptable candidate. Lord Haverly had made it clear that she was a demure lady with a steady disposition.

He had written that she was not at all prone to irresponsible behaviour.

Miss Clarke sat with her hands folded primly in her lap. She did look as if she had the qualities Haverly had stated. Thomas also noted that she was the first candidate his sister had taken the slightest interest in. That, at least, was something. But there was still much he needed to know before he could offer her the position.

Would she be a steadying influence on Minerva? Nothing else really mattered.

'May I ask a question, Miss Clarke?' Minerva enquired before he could speak.

It was hard to miss the relief in Miss Clarke's eyes when his sister spoke. But what was Minerva going to ask? He was half afraid to hear. She had not asked the other ladies anything, in fact had barely smiled at them.

'How do you feel about marriage?'

That was exactly what he was wondering. He held his breath waiting for her answer.

'I think marriage is a wonderful thing.'

Did she? That went in her favour, spoke well of her values.

'As long as both the lady and gentleman both wish it. No woman should be used to promote social standing or family fortune.'

Heaven help him!

'But in society—' He was not able to present his argument because Minerva spoke over him.

'I would like to interview Evie, Thomas. She is to be my companion, after all.'

Evie? Not Miss Clarke? He was beyond help, he

feared. But not so far that he would bury his face in his hands and groan.

This woman was nothing like the kind of companion he had imagined he would hire. With the way her chin dimpled when she smiled, the humour glinting charmingly in her eyes, he had no doubt that eager young fellows would flock to keep company with her. She had an appealing way about her. A way which went beyond simple beauty.

But wait! Perhaps that might go in his sister's favour.

'Do you like animals?' Minerva asked.

'I do. And if you offer me this position, I must say up front that I have a kitten.'

'Oh! That is wonderful!' Minerva clapped her fingertips in excitement, her smile happier than he had seen since he'd brought up the subject of a companion.

'And I assume you would want to have it live here?' he asked.

If he wished to send her on her way this would be his chance to do so. He could claim to be allergic. Of course his sister would point out the lie and embarrass him. He would rather not be embarrassed in front of someone who had a bright dot of pollen on her nose... her pert and pretty nose.

A pert, pretty nose in a lovely face which would draw men in droves.

'Her name is Charm and she will be no trouble at all.'

'I would adore having a kitten to play with and teach to do tricks, if you would allow it, I mean.'

Naturally, Minerva was speaking to Miss Clarke, not to him.

'Charm welcomes attention.' Miss Clarke's smile

was growing more relaxed. Her lips were shapely, quite pretty, really.

He ought to hire her. Surely his sister would be attracted to one of the men attracted to Miss Clarke and her becoming smile. Really, it would be a smart move on his part. The only thing an older companion would give his sister was unwanted advice.

Oh, yes…this young applicant would supply an endless stream of young hopefuls. One of them might change Minerva's opinion of marriage. Having Miss Clarke as Minerva's companion might suit his plans for his sister quite well.

He had his mouth open to offer her the position when Minerva spoke.

'Just one more thing, Evie.' Minerva's eyes were alight with an expression he knew all too well. He was half, no three-quarters, afraid to know what she was going to ask. 'How do you feel about the circus…about circus performers in particular?'

'I have never been to a circus, but I'm sure they are very exciting. When I was young my friend and I made our own circus performances. It was great fun training the estate dogs. We did try the cats, but they did what they wanted to do, not what we wanted them to do.'

Minerva laughed. 'Lambs are the very same way. When I was staying with my brother William on his farm, I tried to get them to jump through a hoop. It was a dim failure.'

Miss Clarke and his sister exchanged a few words about kittens and lambs.

Just because this applicant enjoyed the circus did not

disqualify her. Many people enjoyed attending those extravaganzas.

Then Miss Clarke said the worst thing she could have.

'The best part of our circus was when my father hung a pair of swings in the trees. Mary and I had the grandest of times pretending to be acrobats gliding through the air. We were very young and it was great fun.'

At this point he understood there was no help heaven could give him now. To engage this young woman would be the worst thing he could do, and yet at the same time the best thing.

His imagination exploded. All he could see was the pair of them merrily swinging high up in a circus tent.

'May I also ask you a question, Miss Clarke?'

'But, yes, of course.'

'I hope you do not think it presumptuous of me to ask, but do you see yourself marrying one day?'

'I do not think it presumptuous. My intentions must be of great importance to you.' And then her smile softened. So did her eyes. 'Yes, I would very much like to marry. But only to a man I love and one who loves me. But do rest assured, I will not leave a position any time soon. I am not committed to any man, by love or anything else.'

A part of that answer was what he wanted to hear but a part of it was not. Knowing his sister, she would use Miss Clarke's independent thoughts on marriage as being proof that she herself need not marry.

It was true that not all women had to marry, but they were not a Viscount's only daughter. Minerva certainly did need to marry and for the proper reason. Which was not for love. Love could fail, leaving the couple miserable. He had seen it happen to more than one of his friends. But to wed for the betterment of the family and the title, that was not something that would change. It would always be as it had been in the beginning.

However, Miss Clarke had given a forthright answer. Her letter of recommendation stated that she was of high moral character and honest in her dealings. Honesty was a quality to be highly valued, at least to him it was, and he thought it ought to be to everyone.

He wondered why Haverly had not mentioned how young Miss Evie Clarke was. Not that it mattered… rather, it might be a benefit.

It might matter that his attention kept getting tangled up in her expressive eyes and her playful hair.

Again he reminded himself, she was not to be his companion but Minerva's. Possibly a companion who was as free-thinking as his sister was.

He was fairly certain his father would not approve of engaging a lady whose modern ideas might encourage Minerva to reject marriage more than she already did. Thomas must act as if he were his father in matters involving Rivenhall.

For as much sense as it made to hire Miss Clarke, and as much as he knew his sister wished to have this lady for a companion, he felt he must give the matter due thought. Approach it from every angle.

A mature lady would give Minerva proper guidance, but at the same time she would not help to bring young men flocking to their sides.

What he needed was a few hours to consider everything.

'Miss Clarke,' he stated. 'I do thank you for your time. I shall be in contact with you as soon as I have completed interviewing the candidates.'

Was that a tear that had just sprung to the corner of Miss Clarke's eye? Oh, dash it all, it was!

The last thing he wanted was to make her feel wretched. None of the other ladies he'd interviewed had reacted that way, made him feel a cad. All he had felt in sending them away was frustration at his sister's refusal of them.

Perhaps because none of them had moisture brightening the lovely blue-green shade of their eyes. Nor did they have intriguing curls fighting the captivity of their tidy buns. Not a single one of them had sported an endearing dot of pollen on her nose.

'I shall let you know of my decision later this afternoon, Miss Clarke.'

'Yes, well… I appreciate your consideration.' Why the blazes did her voice have to be quivering? 'It was a pleasure meeting you, Minerva.'

She rose and then walked quickly out of the room, where the butler would be waiting to escort her outside.

Although it was unwarranted, he felt the worst of cads. The dark expression on his sister's face said he was worse than an everyday cad. It was as if she thought he had betrayed her.

Without a word, she snatched the needlework from the floor and sat down on the couch.

Had he betrayed her? It was her future he had in mind. Surely no one could consider this a betrayal.

'Minerva, I shall very likely hire her, but I do have

other ladies to interview. It is only fair to give them their chance.'

Silence. He could not recall a time when she did not have something to say.

'Do you not agree that this is a very big decision we are making and it ought to be given a great deal of thought?'

'I have made my decision.' In a long, slow movement, she drew the red thread through the fabric. 'I suggest you consider what you need to do and do it quickly. You have crushed her feelings.'

The moisture in Miss Clarke's eyes had indicated that something was amiss, but all he had done was conduct an interview. A proper, thoughtful interview.

If she interpreted due consideration as rejection, it was not his fault.

His fault or not, he did feel wicked about the way she'd hurried out of the room. He thought he might have heard a quiet, choked-back sob.

Very well, he would think things over more quickly than he'd meant to.

An older companion might be a more steadying influence. But to imagine she might actually be a companion to Minerva would be wrong. His sister would never be happy spending hours reading books and listening to tales of bygone days. He could not picture it. More likely his sister might—no, would—sneak about in secret doing who knew what.

But Minerva and Miss Clarke shared similar interests and there would be no need to sneak about.

Miss Clarke would tell him what she and his sister did together.

He hoped.

But, yes, she would be upfront with him. Her reference stated quite clearly that she was honest in all her dealings.

The truth was, engaging a companion had been his idea, not his sister's. He ought to be grateful he'd found one she approved of.

It took only seconds to weigh everything up. His decision to employ the pretty companion needed no more thought.

All right then.

He strode after her because there really was no point in waiting until later to offer her employment.

Evie dashed silly tears from her cheeks while she stood on the front porch of Rivenhall. Going down the steps, she could scarcely believe she had reacted so pitifully, so childishly at being refused the position.

The gate gave a soft squeal when she opened it. So did her sense of pride. She felt quite the fool. She would not want to engage her own services after she'd nearly wept out loud.

It was only by the greatest effort that she had not. Her lack of maturity shamed her. If she were to somehow make a go of life in London, she would need to be tougher than that.

Glancing back at the house through a shower of red and gold leaves, seeing the cheerful flowers in the window boxes, she regretted that she would not be living here. It was a beautiful home and she had felt a connection to it before she'd even knocked on the door.

Even more, she regretted that she would not be forming a friendship with Minerva Grant. Truly, she thought they might have become great friends. It would have been such fun to be her companion.

Fun, yes, but a great deal more than that. There was an empty, aching spot in her heart where Mary had been. While she did expect to see her friend again, it was not likely to be for a very long time.

Standing outside the gate, she felt so alone. In this city of thousands, she did not know anyone.

Upon meeting Minerva, she had been hopeful that all would work out rather well. She was certain they would have struck an instant and brilliant friendship.

What was she to do now?

First, she would go to the corner and then stroll for a while. Perhaps she would find a place to have tea. That would settle her nerves. She would take an hour to gather her courage and mentally assess her funds.

She could not stay at the hotel for long. Believing Mary's letter was so glowing that anyone would employ her, she had indulged in taking a room in a very fine place.

Gradually, a sense of resolve replaced despair. And a good thing, too, since she was not used to feeling despair. Having a plan for the very near future, even if it was only for the next hour, she felt her confidence return. After a rallying spot of tea, then a cab back to the hotel, she would enquire about a modest, affordable room to let.

Then she smiled because she was not truly as alone as she thought. Charm was waiting for her. No doubt when the cab dropped her off in front of the inn, she would glance up at her window and find the kitten watching for her return.

Life might not be progressing as she'd hoped it would, but it was progressing without her becoming engaged to Baron Falcon.

Whatever she faced going forward would be better than that.

Chapter Three

Thomas strode towards the front door, regretting that he had not made it clearer to Miss Clarke that he had not rejected her. He could not recall ever bringing tears to a woman's eyes and did not care for the guilt he felt. It had not been his fault, of course. This was business and nothing more.

Still, he would feel better once he made things clear to her.

Luckily, Miss Clarke had made it only as far as the gate. She stood on the pavement looking rather forlorn, glancing about as if she did not know whether to turn left or right.

'Miss Clarke!' he called out while hurrying down the steps. 'One moment, please!' He did not need to turn to know that Minerva was at his heels.

'Mr Grant?' Miss Clarke turned with a pleasant smile. Apparently, she had not been terribly devastated, after all. Or if she had been, she was now recovered.

'I must apologise. I fear I did not make my intentions clear.'

She glanced between him and Minerva, a slight frown dipping her brows. 'I am sure there is no reason to apologise.' To Minerva she said, 'I wish you well, Miss Grant.'

'Please wait, Evie,' Minerva said.

'My sister and I would like to offer you the position of her companion, if you wish to accept it.'

He hoped that she would. And, being the honest man he was, he had to admit that it was not for his sister's sake alone.

The fact of the matter was, it would not be a hardship having such a lovely lady residing at Rivenhall. Her beauty was one of the reasons he was offering her employment, was it not? Surely one of the men she would attract would interest Minerva.

'Please say you will, Evie!' Minerva placed her hands under her chin, looking as if she were in church and desperately praying. 'We will be the best of friends, I am certain we will have the grandest times…as long as you do not enjoy spending useless hours embroidering.'

Evie Clarke smiled, her lips forming the loveliest, most engaging curve. If she accepted, he would be able to see that pretty smile on a daily basis.

Yet it was her hair which caught his attention as much as her smile did. He was curious to know what her curls would do over the course of a day. How many of them would remain captive to the tidy bun when they sat down to dinner each night?

He gave himself a stiff reminder that Miss Clarke was not here to please him, but his sister.

'On my list of favourites, embroidery rates only slightly higher than reading essays.'

'What do you say, Miss Clarke? Will you become a part of the Rivenhall household?' Thomas asked.

'Yes, then. I will happily accept.' It fascinated him to see how the dot of pollen on her nose became more pronounced with the blush softly tinting her cheeks. 'May I say what a beautiful home you have, sir? I will enjoy being here.'

'And we will enjoy having you.' While he said what any gentleman would, he had to admit it would be far more pleasant having her here than any of the other candidates he had interviewed. 'Lord Haverly was glowing in his approval of your qualifications.'

She glanced away. Perhaps she did not enjoy being praised.

For some reason that dot of pollen made him feel a tickle of amusement inside. He had not felt such a sensation in quite some time and it was rather nice.

He should not bring up the pollen, he truly should not, but once in a while an echo of mischief left over from when he was a boy bubbled up. It did not come upon him often, but he felt it nipping at him strongly at that moment.

And so...

'Do you enjoy flowers, Miss Clarke? The scent of them?'

Minerva's shoe slid sideways, kicked his boot.

'But of course.'

He smiled, enjoying the feel of it stretching his lips. At some point over the years, and he was not sure quite when, he had begun to scowl more than he smiled. He pointed to his nose, indicating the spot where hers was dotted in lily pollen.

'Oh, my stars!' Her eyes went wide, and he was struck by how they looked like pools of clear water, neither green nor blue, but some lovely shade in between. She swiped the dust from her nose with the back of her hand. 'Oh, the hazards of horticulture.'

She laughed, wiping her fingers on a handkerchief she withdrew from a small reticule dangling from her wrist.

He hardly knew what to think about the way her smile made him want to give an answering one. It was an odd sensation—pleasant and at the same time uncomfortable.

It was unseemly that he should be so intrigued by his sister's companion. She was now a member of the household—an employee, but at the same time not quite.

And yet what man would not be intrigued by her?

Many of them, he imagined. This had been the main point in hiring her, after all.

He wondered what his father would think of this matter of hiring a companion. But Thomas was in charge of Rivenhall in his father's absence, and in his opinion retaining Evie Clarke was a brilliant move.

'I imagine you have belongings to move to Rivenhall. I will have the carriage brought around. By the time you return, your chamber will be in order.'

Minerva and her new companion exchanged a few words while they all walked back to the house, where he then called for the carriage.

When a short time later the butler announced the carriage ready, the ladies exchanged a hug and a giggle. Apparently they were becoming true companions in quick order.

Now that Minerva had Miss Clarke to keep her company she would be happy while at the same time be guided away from mischief…he hoped.

After Miss Clarke went on her way, Minerva dashed to him, wrapping her arms around his middle in a great hug. 'Thank you, Thomas!'

'You are welcome. It is good to see that you and Miss Clarke are getting along so well…and so quickly.'

She let go of him. Twirled then dashed for the hallway. 'I am going to have Evie's chamber prepared. Is it not grand that we will also have a kitten in the house?'

'We shall see.' He liked kittens, of course, but they also got underfoot. But the house was large and he was not likely to encounter the animal all that often.

He listened to Minerva's footsteps tapping in the hallway. It sounded as if she might be dancing. Then all at once her face peeped back around the door frame.

'And Thomas.' Her grin was too broad, her eyes too glittering. The hairs on his arms prickled. 'When you seek a lady to court, make certain she is not allergic to kittens.'

'A woman to court? What—'

'Do not try and pretend you have forgotten! We made an agreement. I accepted a companion and now you must begin seeking a future Viscountess.'

Well, he had said that. Being a man of his word, he would not go back on it.

Besides, it would put his father's mind at rest to know that his heir was at last doing his duty to Rivenhall in that matter. Anything he could do to help his father recover would be worth the price…and it was said that a merry heart was like a medicine.

'Do you have a lady in mind, Minnie?' No doubt she had a dozen of them.

'Father has always been partial to our neighbour.'

It was true. Lydia Brownton had come up as an example of perfection in the discussions he and his father had engaged in regarding a future Viscountess.

Perhaps she was perfect. Certainly she would do as well as any other well-bred young lady of society, and if she would make his father happy, all the better.

He would begin the process next week…or the one after.

She was not Violet now but Evie, she reminded herself for the tenth or more time since this afternoon—she really must become used to being Evie if she meant to keep her identity a secret.

Even though Rivenhall was a world away from Gossmere she had heard references to this being a small world often enough to feel the need to be cautious.

In truth, she was not being completely dishonest. Violet Evie Clarke Dumel was her name, after all. She had simply changed the order she was using them.

Truly, it was not such an awful thing to do. And yet, not being a person used to being deceitful, she did feel guilty over it. In the end she had done what she needed to do and so she pushed the self-reproach to the back of her mind.

Evie was grateful to have been given this evening to herself in order to settle in and become familiar with her new surroundings.

Thomas Grant had given her permission to freely explore Rivenhall. No place was to be off-limits to her.

He wished for her to feel at home. Oddly enough, she did. It was hard to understand why a place she had never been to before drew her this way, but she could not deny that it did.

Something about the house made her feel safe, even though she was not. She would need to be wary at all times. One never knew who might attend a social event and recognise her. People from Gossmere did travel to London, after all.

Standing beside her open trunk and gazing down at Charm napping in the folds of her nightgown, she was so very grateful that Thomas Grant had agreed to engage her services. She had never been more grateful to be wrong about something. Going out, she had felt sure she had been rejected in favour of another applicant. No sooner had she become reconciled to her fate and considered seeking another path than she was chatting with Minerva about the grand times they would have together.

It only went to show how life could suddenly turn about and one ought not to fall into despair. Even if only for a few moments.

'This room is charming, Charm.' The kitten, having thoroughly explored the space, was now blissfully exhausted by the adventure.

Evie was going to miss her chamber at home and no mistake about it. But change was coming for her, no matter what. At least she had been able to choose its direction.

And the direction she had chosen led her to this cheerful-looking room. It was such a lovely space, she could not help but be pleased.

Glancing about, she felt optimistic that this was going to be a good change. It was hard not to take heart seeing pale blue wallpaper with a pattern of yellow roses tied in white ribbons. Not only that, there were tall glass doors draped with lace curtains, which led to a balcony overlooking a garden.

At home she did not have tall doors leading to a balcony.

While this garden was not the rural countryside she was used to, it was pretty and inviting. She imagined if she went downstairs and took a walk along one of the lantern-lit paths she would not notice the drone of the city even at this time of evening.

The kitten stretched out on a quilt made of blue and yellow squares, yawned and fell promptly asleep again. The flower pattern made it appear that Charm was dozing in a meadow.

'Enjoy it while you can, my friend. As soon as I put my clothes in the wardrobe it will be time for you to go outside.'

Evie hummed while she went about arranging things in their place, thoroughly enjoying the warm snap of the fire that had been laid in the hearth by a smiling young chambermaid. Watching the girl go about her chores so cheerfully indicated that Rivenhall was a pleasant place to live.

There had been a time when Gossmere was a pleasant place to live too. All that had changed when Hubert and Ada had taken it over. More than a few of the staff had resigned rather than serve those harsh, selfish people.

Thomas Grant might be a mostly unsmiling fellow

profile. Although it would have been beyond rude to stare, and him unaware.

He opened his eyes. 'Good evening, Miss Clarke.'

'I beg your pardon. I did not mean to intrude.' Oh, my stars, mean to or not, she felt every inch an intruder…and just when she was beginning to relax and feel at ease here.

'No need to apologise. Visit the garden any time you like. It is meant to be enjoyed.'

She was not certain that he was enjoying it or if he was trying to sort out a problem. A smile would give an indication of his mood, but he did not offer one.

Well, he would have one from her, regardless.

'Thank you. It is very lovely. I came outside to let Charm romp about. When I heard water I simply had to explore.'

The fountain was as pretty as she had thought it would be. But no, cast in moonlight as it was, it was even lovelier than she'd imagined. Water droplets caught the moon's glow and carried it down into the pool. It resembled a drizzle of sparkling crystals.

She hated to walk away so soon after discovering it, but she did not wish to disturb Thomas Grant more than she already had.

'Good evening, then,' she said and turned about to leave him to his solitude.

'May I have a word, Miss Clarke?'

'Yes, naturally.'

He indicated that she should sit down on the bench, so she did. Charm hopped off her lap and vanished into a bush bare of half its leaves.

'I would like to speak to you about my sister…about what I require of your service.'

He looked uncomfortable. But surely not as uncomfortable as she felt. If there was more to this arrangement than being a companion to his sister, he ought to have explained it from the outset.

Now that she was settling in, with a sense that she could be safe and content here, it would be much harder to walk away than it had been earlier today.

Besides, earlier today, Minerva had been a stranger to her. Now that friendship had sparked between them, how was she to abandon that?

Oh, please do not let this be an issue which would force her to leave Rivenhall. Even if it were not for the allowance, she would want to be Minerva's friend. That said, she greatly needed the funds.

She glanced up at the luminous moon. It looked like a great bright ball, hanging in its eternal place no matter what went on down below. She would make it her inspiration. She would hang on, no matter what was revealed in the next few moments.

'Please continue, Mr Grant.'

And please do not let him say that Minerva was deathly ill with some horrid disease.

'I must confess that when I decided to engage a companion I had an older lady in mind. Someone who would have a steadying influence on my sister.'

Evie frowned. Did he think she would not be such an influence? If she knew the man better she might say something to set him straight. But this was not about her but Minerva.

'And you believe she needs it?' It did not seem to

Evie that there was anything unsteady about her new friend. 'To me she seems well adjusted and happy.'

'She is both of those things.'

That was a relief to hear. But she did not understand what he was trying to convey.

'Are you trying to tell me there is something…perhaps not wrong but…well, I do not know what…but something you feel I need to be made aware of? I must say that happy and well-adjusted seems a rather grand state to be in.'

Of course, Minerva's brother would know her far better than she did.

'No, I did not mean to suggest anything was wrong with her. She is quite kind and generous. She greatly resembles our late mother…so does our brother, William.'

It was interesting that he did not include himself as being like their mother who was kind and generous.

But that was a thought for another time. Right now she wished to know his concerns about Minerva.

'But she is also determined to have her way in things and what she wishes for her future is inappropriate.' He stared at his feet in silence and she wondered if he meant to go on.

'Well, unless her heart is set on being a street walker or a thief, I do not imagine it is so awful.' Perhaps she should not speak so forthrightly since she was not well acquainted with him and did not know how he would react to her jest.

He looked up suddenly, a smile twitching one corner of his mouth, but only briefly.

Good then, it was something at least, but it was a

shame he did not smile more often. It was a compelling smile which lit his features, if only for an instant.

'You will recall that she asked you if you enjoyed the circus. This was not a casual enquiry. She has her heart set on becoming a circus performer…what she calls a trapeze artist.'

'Oh!' She laughed, partly in relief and partly because it was quite funny. 'And then I went on about the fun I had as a child. You must have thought me a horrible fit. I am surprised you offered me the position.'

'I believe you will suit my sister nicely.' This time his smile lasted longer, but only by one very nice second.

'Rest assured, sir, I no longer wish to swing from trees or big tops. I have every confidence this is only a passing enchantment on your sister's part.'

'Possibly, but you will soon learn how determined she can be. She does not hesitate to do what she must in order to get her way.'

'Am I to understand that you wish for me to give her guidance? If so, I ought to know which way you would like me to guide her.'

'Towards marriage, naturally. She is a young lady of society and has a duty to wed appropriately.'

'I agree that a future in the circus would be inappropriate. No doubt she would be disillusioned three weeks into it. But I have to say that I believe the choice of a husband is hers to make.'

'And she is welcome to make it…as long as she does make it. And as long as the fellow she chooses is a respectable member of society.'

This was a point she greatly disagreed with him on,

but since she did not wish to jeopardise her position and her allowance, she remained silent on the matter.

Not only that, the poor man looked genuinely troubled by the situation. She would not add to his distress by arguing the merits of female independence. Not now at least…perhaps once they were better acquainted.

It was clear that he wished for her to reassure him that she would guide his sister along the path he wished her to follow. She did not wish to mislead him, but—

'Miss Clarke… I am not saying you are to be a matchmaker, only that I hope you will try to keep her from doing anything which will prevent her from making a good match.'

'As long as she loves the man and he loves her, it will be a good match.'

His brows settled low over his eyes. How interesting that the expression did not detract from his handsome face.

Ordinarily she was drawn to men who smiled easily and laughed often. Something must be wrong with her. Her heart was quite aflutter over a gloomy Tom. Gloomy Tom? Thomas Grant? She nearly chuckled at her witty thought.

It was better that she kept it to herself since she imagined he would not see the humour in it.

She turned her thoughts back to the conversation at hand. Knowing how he felt, she probably should not have spoken up about a lady having a mind of her own when it came to marriage. But really, how could she not?

In Evie's estimation, times were changing. Slowly perhaps, but women were stretching their wings, glancing about and wondering if they might make choices for their future. In the end it would be good for Thomas Grant to accept the fact, given that his sister was one of those women.

However, changing his mind about it was not why she was here. She was here to be a friend to Minerva... that and to hide from Hubert and Baron Falcon.

If that meant keeping quiet about her opinions, so be it.

'Well, sir...' She stood up, smoothed the folds from her skirt and shrugged deeper into the coat because it was growing colder and the wind was frolicsome. 'I should gather up Charm and take her back inside.'

He stood, shivered and stomped his feet. 'It is getting chilly. I will walk back with you.'

He might or might not be enjoying their walk back towards the house. How was she to know? His expression did not indicate one way or another.

Thomas Grant really was not the kind of man who appealed to her and yet somehow...he was. And she was certainly enjoying walking beside him with the fresh scents of the garden being tossed about in the wind, with bare branches rustling in an autumn song.

'Charm!' she called. 'The first time I ever saw her she was dashing about after leaves in the middle of...' Oh, dear...she had better watch what she revealed. 'Of the garden where I was last a companion.'

'Lord Haverly's garden? As I recall, it is quite lovely.'

As he recalled? 'Do you know Lord Haverly?'

'Not well, but we are acquainted. I visited the estate once and found the garden to be quite nice.'

Oh, dear...oh, no! This was not good news.

The small world seemed to be neatly closing in on her. She took a breath, imagined herself being as steady as the moon in its sky. There was nothing to fear as long as Lord Haverly did not come to London.

'Your garden is the most welcoming I have ever seen, sir,' she said, because it was true and also because she wanted to draw the conversation away from Mary's father.

'Would it be too brash if I asked you to call me Thomas? Since we will be living in the same house it seems right.'

Well, yes, it would be brash. At the same time it would be nice. She liked his name. Thomas—it was a strong and in charge sort of name but at the same time friendly.

However, 'As much as I would like to I am not sure it is appropriate.' She stopped and glanced about. 'Where could she have got to?'

Thomas turned this way and that. Suddenly he pointed at a bush. 'There she is, attacking a leaf.'

He hurried over then scooped Charm up in one large hand. The kitten gave a soft meow then licked his thumb.

'Charm, eh?' He handed over the kitten. 'She is that, I suppose.'

They walked for a moment in silence. She hoped he did not feel slighted that she did not call him Thomas. She wanted to, of course.

'I suppose that in private it would do no harm to call you Thomas,' she relented—easily relented, truth to tell. 'But in turn you must call me Evie.'

'Good, then. I shall enjoy using your lovely name.'

He thought her name was lovely? As much as it gave her a small thrill to know it, she could not help but wonder what he would think of Violet.

All too soon they entered the house through the terrace doors. She found she was enjoying strolling along and sharing friendly conversation.

He closed the doors behind them and then nodded at her, stroking Charm's head.

'I hope you have a pleasant night, Evie, and the city noises don't keep you awake. It is very different than in the country.'

'I'm certain I shall become accustomed to it in no time at all.'

'I had trouble sleeping in the quiet when I visited my brother's farm.' He set Charm in her arms. 'Good night, then.'

With another nod, he turned and walked in the opposite direction. She had yet to learn where everything was in this vast house. Luckily she did know the way back to her chamber.

Hurrying inside her room, she set the kitten on the floor in front of the hearth. She removed her clothes and put on her nightgown.

Once in bed she did not fall asleep straight away, as she'd imagined she would. It had been a long, eventful day and she was exhausted. She ought to be dreaming by now.

But she was dreaming…daydreaming at night. Of Thomas Grant's rare and very nice smile.

Chapter Four

Thomas walked in Hyde Park, several paces behind Minerva and Evie. He rolled his shoulders, enjoying the feel of sunshine penetrating his coat and warming his back.

An hour ago he had been in the study, looking over ledgers, when Minerva had burst into the room begging him to accompany her and Evie on a walk before tea. He had resisted at first. He had a duty to make sure the accounts were in order and did not wish to shirk it.

But in the end here he was, and glad for it. Autumn was in the air; a burst of colour tinted the foliage. The breeze was not as brisk as last night, but it was still fresh and bracing.

He was far enough behind his sister and her companion that he could not hear what they were saying, but they were clearly delighted to be in one another's company.

All at once Evie laughed. What a pretty sound it was. It tickled his heart, made it smile, if a heart could do such a thing.

After their conversation in the garden last night he felt reassured that she would be good for Minerva.

And good for him as well. If he needed to ask Evie a question about Minerva he believed she would answer him truthfully.

Now that he was feeling more confident of Minerva's situation he could turn his attention to his own. What better place to begin looking at ladies in the light of a future Viscountess than the park where several of them were taking the air?

While it was very likely to be Miss Brownton he would court, it could not hurt to consider other ladies too.

Here came one now, strolling with her mother on the left and her aunt on the right. He knew Miss Johnstone. She was a small, frail lady who tended to blend into any setting. He did not think she would be a good match for Rivenhall.

They walked past a bench where he spotted Lady Smythe. She sat with an older lady he thought must be her companion, neither of them were smiling or speaking. What had ever made him think his sister would have been happy with a sober older woman to keep her company? Seeing the ladies walking ahead of him, he was grateful Miss Clarke had accepted the engagement.

And as for Lady Smythe becoming his wife? No... he could not see it. Lady after lady walked past and he could not imagine any of them in the role.

After an hour, he suggested it was time to return home for tea.

Shadow and sunshine shifted across the path in front

of them. The breeze lifted the hem of his coat while he turned his search inward.

The search did not last long before it settled on the obvious lady. Miss Lydia Brownton had long been his father's favourite and for good reason.

As the daughter of a viscount she would have been well prepared for stepping into the role she would play as his wife. As his father often pointed out, Lydia had never been the subject of gossip. Thomas could not recall her ever laughing too loudly or speaking out of turn. A more demure, respectable lady would be hard to find.

But, having made the decision, he did not wish to be hasty in beginning a courtship. The choice of a marriage partner was a rather important one. He would need time to give it due consideration.

Had his father not been ill, he might have dragged his feet on the matter of marriage even longer. Now, fearing he might become Viscount much sooner than he wanted to, he needed to have the matter settled.

He would pray every night that his father would recover. In the meantime he would carry on as if…well, he could not think of it.

It was time for him to wed, regardless of circumstances.

Perhaps he might host a dinner party and invite several families with daughters. This would give him a chance to consider Lydia more closely without singling her out before he was ready to. It was important to determine if she would suit him…or, more importantly, Rivenhall before society was aware of his intentions.

By inviting several ladies and their families, no one would suspect what he was up to.

Well, then, he felt rather pleased with this plan.

Even better, he could invite young men of marriageable age. They would be keen to meet Evie and flock about her. If Minerva's companion enjoyed their attentions, perhaps his sister would look at suitors in a better light.

This might be wishful thinking on his part. There was every chance that Evie would not welcome their attention. But, upon occasion, wishes did come true.

And sometimes what one wished for did not happen but something better did. Engaging Evie Clarke instead of a more mature lady was an example.

It was time, he decided, to become more flexible in his outlook on life. A less rigid view might gain him what he wanted more easily than seeing only one way towards a goal.

In the case of Minerva's companion, more pleasant certainly.

Watching Evie, seeing her feminine stride and her delight at catching a falling leaf in her hand, made him smile.

Not only on the inside.

Another lady might catch a leaf, but he could not imagine himself smiling over it. Would he smile if Miss Brownton caught a leaf?

It would be nice to smile at her, he decided, but not essential. But it was essential to host a dinner party to consider Rivenhall's future Viscountess.

Evie strode down the short hallway leading to Thomas's study.

It had been two days since he'd accompanied her and

Minerva on a walk in the park. The weather had been delightful, as well as getting to know Minerva better. Hearing what she had to say about the people passing by had been interesting.

But more interesting than anything else had been Thomas's presence. Not that he'd walked with them, but several paces behind. It was the oddest sensation, but Evie had felt it every time his attention lingered on her back.

What had he been thinking? Hopefully he approved of her conduct as his sister's companion. It was a tricky business, balancing what he required of her with what Minerva wished of their friendship. But she had an idea to present to him regarding Minerva's wish to become a circus performer.

Seeing his closed door, her stomach fluttered nervously. No doubt it was due to anticipation of his approval of what she proposed. It was certainly not due to remembering how she had felt when she knew his eyes were upon her while walking in the park. Flutters could be caused by any number of things.

Could they not?

She hesitated for a second before knocking on the study door.

This was the perfect time to present what she considered a brilliant plan. Hopefully, he would think it was too. With Minerva away visiting friends, Evie had been given the day off and was now free to speak with Thomas privately.

All right, then. She pressed her stomach with one hand and rapped on the door with the other.

She heard a chair scrape, footsteps cross the floor. The door opened. The flutters beat madly in her chest.

'Evie…hello. Please come in.' He swept his arm in a gesture to welcome her inside.

Rain beat on a tall window behind the desk. There was a fire blazing in the hearth. He indicated that she should sit in one of the chairs in front of it.

Thomas started to go to the desk, but then turned about and took the chair across from her.

'Is there something I can do for you, Evie?'

He could smile—that would make her feel more reassured about presenting her idea. There was every chance that he would refuse. At the same time, if he did not refuse and they acted upon her idea there was every chance it could go terribly wrong.

Her judgement would be brought into question. She could be dismissed if this did not work.

'It concerns your sister.'

His frown dipped, half hiding the expression in his eyes…but only half.

'Has she got into trouble?'

'Oh, no…not at all.'

'I am glad to hear it. But you are getting along well? It seems that you are.'

'We are becoming true friends.'

'I thought so.' And there it was, a brief smile dancing on his lips, shining out of his eyes.

It was lucky the expression passed quickly or she might have forgotten what she had come to say. There was no denying the source of the flutters this time. It was completely inappropriate. She must simply ignore the fact that, for some reason, Thomas Grant's smile went straight to her heart.

Soon there was to be a dinner party. Minerva had told her that the occasion was being held for Thomas to begin a bride search.

One thing was for certain, he would not be searching for her. According to Minerva it would be their neighbour, Lydia Brownton.

She must have been silent for too long, woolgathering where she ought not to, because Thomas lifted his brows as if in anticipation of what she had come to say.

'I have an idea. One which might diminish the glamour of circus life. It might convince Minerva to direct her attention towards something else.'

'Are you perhaps a miracle-worker, Evie?'

If only she was! She would still be at Gossmere with her parents and Mary.

Although if that were true she would not be here sitting across from Thomas Grant. Since the past could not be changed, being here was not an awful place to be.

She shook her head. 'I have an idea only.'

He nodded, encouraging her to carry on with it.

'I suggest we take Minerva to a circus and let her see first-hand what it is like. That it is not all glamour.'

'She might find it to her liking and see only what she wants to see.'

'Perhaps, if we take her to the Wild West Show that would be the case. It is rather impressive.'

'I have managed to keep her away from it. Luckily it closes this month. If Minerva ever saw a lady sharpshooter she would pack her bag and move to America.'

'I was thinking of one with a less than sterling reputation. Perhaps you know of one?'

He nodded, arching a brow. 'There is Frenchy's Big Top Extravaganza. I have heard bad things about it. This could work.'

'It will work…or make her even more starry-eyed.' He had been correct to think it might.

'We shall simply point out the ugly parts without her knowing what we are doing.'

'I hope we can. She is very bright and might see through it.'

'Even if she does suspect it, she cannot ignore what she sees.'

She might do so. But Evie thought this might work. She only hoped that she would not be risking their new friendship if Minerva discovered her intentions.

'We shall do it, Evie. Let us shake hands on our success.' He stared at his offered hand, lifted his brows for an instant then clenched his fist as if he were surprised he had offered it. 'But perhaps I overstep.'

Touching hands would be overstepping, on both their parts. And yet everything she had been doing of late was bold so…well, what harm could it do?

She extended her hand. He uncurled his fingers and wrapped them around hers.

'Yes, let's hope for it. Success in our endeavour.'

He did not squeeze, or linger overlong, but long enough for her to feel how strong and manly those long fingers were. The butterflies in her belly returned with a vengeance. She had never touched a man's hand before and it was…my word, it was interesting.

Fascinating.

If Mary were here they would giggle over it. As it was, she would be keeping this reaction to herself. She could not discuss Minerva's brother with her, after all. That would not be fitting.

Thomas released her hand, his smile confident of success and…she could not deny what her eyes saw… very handsome. Funny how the butterflies continued to batter about her belly.

'If the rain stops we shall go tomorrow evening. Unless you and my sister have other plans?'

'We are to shop for new hats in the early afternoon, but after that we are free.'

'Until tomorrow, then,' he said with a nod.

Apparently, having discussed her business, she was now dismissed. Unlike her tingling fingers. The sparkling feeling in them was not about to be dismissed.

Rising, she returned his nod. 'Until tomorrow.'

It should not bother her to be sent on her way so formally. She was not his companion, after all. They were friendly, but at the heart of it, theirs was a business relationship.

She clasped her hands together at her waist, squeezing her fingers together to make it known to them.

She must not forget he was about to begin searching for a wife. According to Minerva, this was business too. His heart was not leading the way, but rather obligation.

Poor Thomas. She did feel sorry for him. But in the end it was not for her to point out there was a better reason to marry than because it was expected of one.

Tall torches lined the walkway leading into the big top. Music beckoned ticket-holders to enter, to leave their everyday lives behind and get lost in the spell-binding world within.

Coming inside, Thomas led his sister and Evie to the benches. If one did not look too closely, one might believe the circus to be an island of enchantment. Colourful banners were draped across the performance rings, swaying from the towers acrobats would climb to perform fearful feats of derring-do.

Children clung to their parents' hands when clowns got too close. Then parents clung to their children's hands when a trio of poodles dyed pink and wearing tutus paraded past.

'Let's sit on top where we can see everything!' Minerva exclaimed and then dashed up the steps.

She looked as happy as any of the children making their way in and finding their places on the benches. While his sister was a woman grown, she was delightfully young at heart. He had to admit loving that quality in her even though it worried him at times...many times.

Minerva took a spot on the end of the bench, Evie sat beside her and then he took the place next her. With so many people there, they were squeezed hip to hip.

There were a dozen smells under the big top, but the scent that caught his attention was lavender. It was coming from Evie. Every time her posture shifted, the delicate fragrance wafted up to him.

'This is the most thrilling thing that has ever happened to me!' Minerva's smile could barely be contained on her face.

'Better than when Elizabeth had her babies?'

Minerva had been delirious with joy over their happy entrance into the world.

'That was an entirely different thing and you know it. Nothing will ever be as grand as holding the twins.' She clapped her hands when an elephant entered the largest of the rings. 'But, Thomas, even you must admit how magical this all is.'

'It is quite glittering.' He did have to agree with that much.

Then he whispered to Evie, 'The tent canvas is filthy...did you notice?'

She nodded, clapping along with Minerva. Once again the scent of lavender came to him, delicate and in no way overpowering like the perfumes some ladies used.

'I noticed something that was probably vile smeared on the door flap. And there is an odd scent in the air,' she said.

'I'm not sure Minerva will see through the glamour.' He leaned closer to her ear so that his sister would not hear his whisper. Another scent filled his nose...his senses. Under the lavender she smelled utterly feminine. He forgot what he meant to say for a second. 'I fear this is going to gain the opposite result than I hoped for.'

'Never fear, Thomas, we shall succeed in the end.'

It struck him, her casual use of the term 'we'. It made him feel that he had an ally. Knowing that Evie Clarke was on his side in this matter was reassuring.

A spot in his heart felt thoroughly warmed, as if touched by a...well, a kiss was what came to mind, but that was wrong.

'Look how smart the sweet little poodles are!'

'And pink,' Thomas muttered to Evie.

'I think they look frightened,' she answered.

'Oh, no...' Minerva shook her head. 'I am certain they are only intent upon showing off their tricks and then receiving a treat for their efforts.'

'The elephant does not look all that happy either,' he pointed out.

'I do not know how you can tell whether an elephant is happy or not. Their natural look is rather solemn,' Minerva said. His sister gasped, stood up and clapped when the elephant stood on his hind legs and trumpeted. 'He is magnificent!' she declared, sitting once again.

Evie leaned close to whisper, 'I would rescue the poor beast if I could.'

Being so close, her thigh brushed his. He felt the shapeliness of it even under yards of clothing.

'Oh, look! Here come the trapeze artists! Oh, thank you for bringing me, Thomas. This might be the best night of my life...aside from the babies being born.'

Evie glanced up at him and blinked.

He blinked back.

She must also suspect they were failing miserably in their mission.

Once the acrobats began to perform he knew the cause was lost—his sister seemed more enchanted by the people flying about in the top of the tent than she had ever been.

He heard his sister using words like 'heavenly', 'ethereal', 'magical' and 'angelic'.

Being close together on the bench, he felt it when

Evie sighed. Under the cover of her billowing skirt, she gave his hand a quick squeeze.

The gesture both surprised and delighted him. Perhaps she did not consider it such a bold thing to do since they had touched hands before. Was this time so much different than that? On both occasions it had been in the cause of saving Minerva from a wrong decision.

Ah, but he had never been touched quite this way before, except by his mother when he was a young child. But there was a quality to her touch that warmed and startled him all in one silent leap of his heart.

While Minerva was caught up in admiration of her idols, Evie leaned close…oh, so close…to whisper in his ear. 'I have an idea. Please go along with it.'

'Very well.' He hoped he would not regret it.

He watched in silence while the acrobats thrilled the crowds by not falling to their deaths.

'Minerva…' Evie whispered something to his sister, but he could not tell what it was.

'My brother will forbid it.' He did hear that and it gave him a chill up his neck. But Evie had asked him to trust her and he supposed he must.

'Thomas, Evie and I must be excused for an urgent matter,' Minerva said.

'What urgent matter?' His sister would expect him to question it.

'To use the facilities, if you must know.' Minerva sighed in clear exasperation at needing to explain.

'If you must,' he answered. 'But hurry back.'

Rising, Evie gave him a quick wink.

Silently, he wished her luck because he feared coming here had been a great blunder.

* * *

It was a risky thing to attempt. Evie was not at all certain it was even possible to get behind the big tent, where she hoped the tawdry side of the circus would be revealed. And if she did manage to get there without being discovered, would it be as ugly as she imagined? And if it was, would Minerva recognise it through the stars in her eyes?

At the thought of stars in the eyes, Evie had to shake them out of her own. What had come over her to touch…squeeze…Thomas's hand…again? If it were anyone else she would never have done such a thing.

But it was Thomas, and in that moment they had been sharing a secret…a bond of sorts.

Still, perhaps she should not have done it. Hopefully this misadventure would not prove to be something else she should not have done.

'This way.' Minerva tugged on her sleeve.

They followed an unlit but well-worn path that led from the rear of the tent then through a growth of trees. There was an odour here…probably from the animals not being cleaned up after.

Not surprisingly, the path emerged at what looked like animal cages.

Evie pinched her nose to relay the message that the area smelled awful. Minerva gave her the same gesture back.

A short distance beyond the cages were the performers' wagons. Creeping quietly along, she listened for someone to shout a warning for them to halt.

No one did. One would think—hopefully Minerva did at least—that someone as valued as a trapeze artist would be guarded from nosey intruders such as themselves.

The scent of a cigar overpowered the unpleasant odour of the animal cages. Evie did not care for the smell of cigars, but it was better than what they had left behind.

Hearing voices, one a woman's and one a man's, they tiptoed that way. Coming around the corner of wagon, they came up short.

One of the fairylike performers sat on the steps of a wagon, a lamp illuminating the space around her. A fat brown cigar hung from her lips. Whoever she had been speaking to was no longer present, but his grumbling voice could be heard fading in the darkness.

Up close, the acrobat was not as lovely as she had seemed on her swing. But that might be because of the cigar and the ring of smoke curling around her head. The lady had a hardened look to her, one that spoke of a difficult life. Evie had thought this would be the case, which was why she'd brought Minerva out here.

Possibly, the lady never had a father or a brother to protect her, the way Evie and Minerva had.

'You fine ladies lost?' the woman asked, not bothering to clear her mouth of the obstruction.

'Well, no, miss.' Minerva stepped closer. Evie kept close by her side. 'We have come to meet you and tell you how amazing your performance is.'

When the woman laughed, it was a harsh sound which ended in a coughing fit.

'Caught in the glamour of it all, are you? You aren't the first. Won't be the last either.'

'I hope to become a trapeze artist myself. It is my greatest dream.'

At that the woman dropped the cigar and ground it in the dirt with her slipper.

'Your dream, my nightmare.' The woman actually snorted.

Minerva gasped, but very quietly. 'But you must have the most wonderful life, so exciting and thrilling.'

'I risk my neck every night and for what? To hear the applause? No, for the money…which amounts to dirt anyway, if you want to know.'

'With your skills I would think you could ask for any amount of money,' Evie suggested.

She was sorry to see Minerva's surprise and disappointment, but at the same time relieved.

'You would think so, but no.' The woman cast a scornful calculating glance over both her and Minerva. Out of admiration for the circus, Minerva had worn her very best gown. 'I'm only a step away from walking the streets as it is. And if you think hanging onto that swing is amusing…think again, missies. My hands are raw.' She opened her palms in the lamplight for them to see. 'My joints ache and I fear every moment that I will fall to my death or be crippled.'

'I am truly grieved to hear it,' Minerva muttered, her expression crushed.

'I wonder…have you ever feared where your next meal would come from? I rather doubt it. More like where your next hat will come from, I'd say.'

Minerva was wearing the cheerful yellow bonnet they had purchased today.

'I promise you, that hat is something I can only

dream of having...' The woman's glance at the hat seemed balanced between yearning and scorn. But Evie thought it understandable, given the difference in the life she must have led and the lives she and Minerva did lead. 'I will tell you the truth, same as I tell other starry-eyed ladies sneaking back here. This is not the life for the likes of you. Go along with you now, before Freddie comes back and finds you here. He's a surly sort and doesn't like people poking around.'

'Shall we call the constable, miss?' Minerva asked. 'If he mistreats you he—'

'Oh, now, it wouldn't do to have our prince arrested, would it?'

Minerva untied the ribbon under her chin, handing her new hat to the woman.

'Let's go, Evie.' Minerva gripped her hand, seeming in a hurry to be away from here. But at the edge of the lamplight she turned about. 'I would just like to say that your performance was wonderful.'

Another lady dressed in a performer's costume came out of the trailer, staring at them with what could only be envy edged with contempt.

'Come, Minerva,' Evie whispered. 'Let's go before your brother misses us and comes looking.'

Hand in hand, they walked quickly away, but not quickly enough not to overhear. 'I got myself a hat out of that one.'

Poor Minerva must be crushed to her soul. Evie felt wicked for having shown her the ugly truth. It had been necessary, of course, but she greatly regretted how her friend must be feeling.

Approaching the animal pens, the foul odour returned. An angry cursing voice broke over the sounds coming from the big top. A dog yelped and then another whined.

It sounded as if someone was mistreating the dogs. The acrobats' prince? What an awful man this Freddie must be.

'The acrobats might refuse help—' Evie's breath felt hot hissing past her lips '—but we will do what we can for the poodles.'

When she would have rushed towards the dog pen, Minerva yanked her back into the shadows.

'Wait until he goes away,' she whispered.

The man dropped a handful of what she imagined to be meat on the earthen floor of the cage. The pups did not approach their dirty meal until the awful man left the cage.

'I have changed my mind about joining the circus,' Minerva said, leading the way towards the cage.

Thomas would be greatly relieved.

'I shall now rescue mistreated animals.'

And clearly she meant to begin right now.

She unlatched the cage door, going down on her knees. She opened her arms to the dogs and made kissing noises.

At first the dogs hung back, hesitant to approach, but then one of them crept forward to sniff Minerva's hand. When it seemed as if the small beast trusted her, she picked it up, cooed over it and then handed it to Evie.

'There's one we can get away from here.' Minerva went down on her knees again to tempt another cowering dog to come to her.

Glancing up over her shoulder, she gasped and cried out.

In the same instant, a heavy hand clamped down on Evie's shoulder. She looked up and back. Oh, no! It was the man who had mistreated the dogs.

'Freddie?' Who else could it be?

'We don't take kindly to thieves around here…there's a price to pay.'

The way he laughed sent a chill through her.

'Put the dog down,' he ordered, his chuckle as ugly as he was.

'Brute!' Minerva shouted. 'If you do not let go of her I shall free the other dogs!'

Chapter Five

Thomas had an uneasy feeling in his gut. He was not certain exactly what Evie had in mind when she took his sister to 'use the facilities' but he feared it would not end well.

They ought to have returned by now. If harm came to them it would be his fault. He should never have brought Minerva here, nor should he have allowed her and Evie to go off on their own.

He stood suddenly, startling the gentleman seated beside him. There was no help for it. He was responsible for Minerva and Evie. No harm would come to them on his watch. He would not allow it.

Rushing out of the tent, he glanced about. Which way would they have gone?

Since Evie's intention had been to point out the seedy side of the circus, she would probably have gone to the living quarters of the performers. If she meant to prove to his sister that the circus, especially the life of a performer, was not all glitter and glamour, that was where she would find the evidence.

Behind the tent he spotted a path leading through a copse. He raced along it.

'Put the dog down,' he heard, then a man's snide laughter.

'Brute!' Oh, dash it! That was Minerva shouting. 'If you do not let go of her I shall free the other dogs!'

'Release me!' Evie cried.

It was impossible to miss the pain in her voice. Red-hot rage pumped through him in a way he had never felt before.

He broke into the clearing, rushing into an area scattered with animal cages. He heard a growl coming from one of them. Perhaps it was not a tiger making the sound, but himself.

'The prettier the thief the harsher the penalty.'

The man's back was to him. Intent as he was on threatening Evie, it was unlikely he noticed Thomas hurrying between the unkempt cages.

Evie squirmed under the man's grip. A roar threatened to escape Thomas's throat, seeing how his fingers dug into her shoulder. He held the searing sound in, meaning to take the man by surprise.

Minerva rushed to help Evie, her fingers flexing as if she intended to rip the villain apart with her fingernails.

'Get back!' Thomas shouted at her, closing the distance.

Clearly startled, the man turned towards him without releasing his grip on Evie.

Thomas punched him in the chin. The man fell on his knees, stunned and gasping.

'Let's go,' he said.

'But the dogs! We must take them with us!' Minerva held open the cage door, waving for them to come out.

'The constable will haul you all to jail for the theft of valuable property,' the despicable creature on the ground moaned.

'You do not treat them like valuable property!' Evie accused, pressing the dog in her arms closer to her heart.

'As loathsome as he is—' Thomas pinned the man with a glare when he started to rise; that was interesting, he'd never realised his glare was so persuasive, it must have been the punch lending it authority '—he is correct. We cannot take the dogs. It would be theft.'

'Rescue, more like. I'm pretty sure he was beating them.' Minerva looked as if she was about to deliver a swift kick to the miserable lout.

'Minerva! We are leaving here now.'

'But—'

'Now.' He gathered Evie under one arm then Minerva rushed under his other.

'If this lady is bruised,' he snarled, 'it is you who will face the constable.'

'Oh, Thomas,' Minerva said while he hustled them back towards the big top. 'You should punch him again. It was ever so grand and heroic.'

'Do you still wish to join this group of miscreants?' he asked, hurrying them past the tent entrance. Torch flames danced in the dark, looking hellish rather than magical as they had earlier. 'If you do, I forbid it.'

It was a relief to see the Rivenhall carriage waiting beside the kerb only a short distance up the street.

Thomas hurried the ladies along and then, without

waiting for the driver to assist, handed them up into the carriage.

Glancing over his shoulder to make certain they had not been followed, he climbed in after them. He felt half sick to his stomach, understanding too late the danger he had allowed them to walk into.

'You do not need to forbid me, brother. I have turned my attention to something more worthy.'

She did not say what it was and this was not the moment to enquire. He barely held onto his patience as it was. Tomorrow he would ask Evie. She would tell him the truth.

Because of tonight's misadventure, he felt a bond of some sort had been forged between him and Evie. He trusted that they were allies in securing Minerva's future.

It seemed that the day had gone on for ever. Evie had spent the entirety of it accompanying Minerva to shops in the morning and visits in the afternoon.

All she had wanted from the moment she'd risen this morning was to have a private word with Thomas. Either he had been out or she had, so it had not happened.

She could only imagine how upset he must be after she'd got his sister in such a spot last night. He was clearly protective of Minerva and what had Evie done? Delivered her smack into the midst of trouble.

She must speak with him, although she feared as soon as he saw her she would be dismissed. A tingle skittered over her nerves, just imagining what would have happened had Thomas not come looking for them.

As much as she would like to deny it, she had been

wrong to sneak Minerva out behind the big top. And then to try and take the dogs! What on earth had come over her?

'Come along, Charm. It is time for you to take care of your business before dinnertime.' She scooped the kitten up and carried her down to the garden.

Stepping outside, the wind whipped and whistled. Luckily, there was a large conservatory in the garden where all three of the garden paths met. She picked the shortest one and hurried along it. Along the way she fortified herself to ask Thomas for a moment of his time.

Immediately after dinner she was going to do it. She would lay her future employment upon his mercy.

'It really was an irresponsible thing to do,' she explained to Charm. 'Oh, but you should have seen those poor dogs. And if you want to know, the people who work for that circus were treated little better. I promise, you will never encounter anyone like that horrid Freddie.'

Coming inside, she closed the door quietly behind her, set Charm down and then gazed out at the garden through the glass. With the sun going down, it was neither light nor dark.

Twilight was so very soft on the senses. What an enchanting time of day.

Watching the branches blow and leaves scatter, she wished she could go back and change what she had done last night, avoid putting herself and Minerva in danger.

However, a couple of things about last night had been wonderful. Sitting close to Thomas on the bench had been one of them. Arm to arm, hip to hip… Well, it was distracting in quite a pleasant way.

Would she feel that way about any man she sat so close to, or was Thomas special? She had no way of knowing for certain since she had never sat so close to a man before, but she thought...

Thought nothing, since Thomas Grant was not hers to think about. Indeed, he was about to begin courting a lady who was his neighbour.

Oh, but then again, who could not think about a man who rescued her from the clutches of a villain...ripped her right out of his grip then punched him, knocked him on his backside. He had been her hero, made her feel all fluttery inside, even given what had happened.

She rolled her sore shoulder. There was a bruise under her gown, but it would have been much worse had Thomas not raced to their defence.

'Does it hurt?'

She spun around at the voice coming from the shadows.

Thomas!

A row of torches outside the conservatory shed enough light within to reveal his silhouette striding towards her. Without question, her hero was as handsome as he had been last night. She suspected he would always be her hero, even if it was in the secrecy of her mind.

She had never been rescued from anything before and it made her feel...she was not sure what, but cherished perhaps. Or fired from her position, there was that probability.

But she gave a great sigh at seeing him standing before her. Again she did this in the privacy of her heart.

'Not horribly.'

'Will you sit with me for a moment?'

There was a bench near the window which he indicated with a sweep of his hand.

And here it came—the termination of her employment. While she sat, she straightened her shoulders, readying her heart to be courageous, her attitude gracious in the face of the certain setback of her situation.

'I apologise for—' she said.

'Thank you for—' he said at the same time.

And then in unison, 'Last night.'

'But why—?'

Once again they spoke over each other.

And then the most wonderful thing happened. Thomas Grant gave her a full, bright smile. The spark of humour carried all the way to his eyes.

'Please, Evie, you speak first.'

'Actually, I have been hoping to speak to you all day but the opportunity did not present itself.'

She glanced about for Charm. Curiosity must have lured her away on an exploration, but surely she was safe inside the conservatory.

'What was it you wished to speak to me about? I have been hoping to speak with you as well.'

His smile fell a bit, curving up on only one side. It would have felt wickedly awful facing his full smile when he let her go.

'I only wish to say how sorry I am to have led your sister into a situation where she could have been injured. It was the worst judgement on my part.'

'Please, Evie, do not look so distressed. I only wish to give you my thanks. It seems that Minerva has got over her desire to risk her life on the trapeze.'

Shade by shade, the night beyond the glass grew darker and wind blew the flames in the torches nearly sideways.

Hope that she was not about to be sent packing rallied her spirits. She did not wish to leave Rivenhall, Minerva…or Thomas, to be completely honest about it.

She was coming to like him rather well.

'I appreciate it more than you know, putting yourself in harm's way for the sake of my sister.'

'I did not expect to encounter Freddie. Only to watch from a distance so that Minerva could see first-hand what the life of a circus performer was.' She shivered under her coat. 'I discovered more than I thought I would.'

'I am sorry about leaving the dogs behind. But truly, there was no way we could do anything to help them.'

'You are right. Of course. I think Minerva and I got caught up in the heat of a righteous cause.'

'And speaking of causes, she mentioned a new one. Am I to understand rescuing helpless creatures, is it?'

She hesitated for a moment. As Minerva's companion, her loyalties lay with her. It was not her place to reveal all Minerva's secrets. Although she did understand her brother's desire to be protective, she would not betray her friend's trust.

'I apologise. It sounds as if I am asking you to report her behaviour to me. I do not wish to put you in a difficult place. The truth is, I am happy to see the two of you getting along so well.'

'Minerva is a wonderful friend. And you are right. I will not betray her trust, but if you have any concerns and I may ease your mind, I will be happy to do so.'

'That is reassuring. I will admit, it has been something of a challenge keeping her in line during Father's absence. Because of you, he will not return to find her swinging in the big top wearing…' He paused, frowned and shrugged.

'I am grateful for your understanding, Thomas. I was afraid you were going to send me away for what happened last night. It did end in a mess.'

'I take the blame for it. I should not have permitted you to go off alone. Again, I am sorry for it.' Charm meowed from somewhere in the conservatory. 'I will admit to being concerned that you were going to resign. The thought wore at me all day.'

Would he be unhappy if she resigned? The butterflies plaguing her recently fluttered their precocious little wings.

'With your guidance, Minerva might yet find a man to court,' he said.

Of course, there was nothing personal in him worrying that she would leave Rivenhall. She ought not to have thought so.

'If she finds a young fellow she wants to court I will support her. But, on the other hand, well, you are aware of how I feel about being forced to wed. I will support her choice not to wed as well.'

'May I speak frankly, Evie?'

'Of course, there is no reason in speaking otherwise.'

'Minerva, as the daughter of a Viscount, is required to marry for the good of Rivenhall. Surely you know that. Not that I wish her to be miserable. I want her to have every happiness, and yet I am confident she will find it with an appropriate young man.'

Not all suitors were young, many of them not appropriate, she thought, but she did not wish to reveal anything about her own situation and so kept quiet, steering the conversation away.

'I wish the same for you, Thomas. I hope you will find every happiness with an appropriate young lady.' Yes, indeed she did—it was only right to hope that for him.

'I imagine Minerva has spoken to you of the reason for the dinner party next week?'

'She did mention it.' If she told him all of what his sister had mentioned, how would he react? There was but one way to know. 'As I understand it, there was an agreement between you. If she engaged a companion, you would begin looking for the future Lady Rivenhall.'

'It was an easy bargain since I need to do so anyway.' He sent her a half smile. 'My father has been encouraging me to take the step for a while now.'

'Is it what you wish to do?'

'I wish to be a proper Viscount one day. My father is ill and so there is some pressure to live up to my duty.'

'I am so sorry to hear Lord Rivenhall is not well. I pray it is nothing terribly serious.'

'He is on holiday in Scotland to aid his recovery so I would think not... But when it comes to illness it is hard to know. I also pray all will be well.'

Illness could be long and lingering. Or it could strike quickly and rob someone of both her parents in the blink of an eye. It could break one's heart little by little or all at once.

This was not something she could dwell on at the moment. Not without risking weeping in front of Thomas, not if she wished to make him worry more about his father.

'It is honourable of you to live up to your duty.' At the cost of your own happiness, she thought. Honourable, yes, and foolish.

'I believe in honour…and duty even more. My duty is to wed an appropriate lady. Minerva's duty is to wed an appropriate gentleman.'

Poor Thomas. Many people would envy his place in society, but as far as Evie was concerned the cost was far too great.

Certainly, Minerva would not be willing to pay it.

'I believe the dinner will be successful, Thomas. As long as Miss Brownton holds the same ideals that you do when it comes to marriage.'

'You know about Lydia? But of course Minerva would have mentioned her.'

'Your sister and I have become quite close, so yes, she does tell me things.'

'What does she tell you about Lydia?'

'Are you sure you wish to know?'

'Not at all sure, but…' He shrugged, gazing intently at her.

'Your sister says that Lydia Brownton is a perfectly acceptable choice.'

'Good then. I am glad she approves.'

There was a bit more to it, and he had asked, so…

'But she does not approve…not right now at least. She is withholding her complete opinion until she has seen the two of you together in a courting situation.'

'I hope she approves of what she sees since they will be sisters.'

'She likes Miss Brownton well enough. But you must know that in your sister's estimation an appropriate match does not equal a happy one. She wants very much to see you happy, Thomas.'

'And what do you think? Would an appropriate match make a man like me happy?'

A man like him? Well, that made her think. A handsome man, a devoted and brave man...one with honour and duty embedded in his bones?

He seemed to believe he would be happy with an 'arrangement'. How could she believe it when, in unguarded moments, she had felt his smile warmly resting upon her? No, there was more to this man than he presented, and so she thought he might not be happy.

She could not say so, but he deserved much more than he was likely to get in the kind of marriage he envisaged. No wonder he had postponed the bride search for so long. What he might not realise was that, deep in his soul, he wanted something more.

But perhaps there would be a special spark between him and Miss Brownton. She hoped so for his sake. But they had been neighbours for many years. Had there been an attraction, surely he would have begun courting her long ago.

'I cannot say whether it would or not. You know how I feel, Thomas. There is only one good reason to wed and that is for love. I dearly hope that you find it with the lady you choose.'

This conversation was becoming rather intimate. Thomas had only meant to thank Evie for what she had done last night. Speaking of personal things, especially with a near stranger, was not something he was comfortable with. Although there was something about Evie Clarke. Even knowing her for such a short time, she did not feel like a stranger.

She had a quality about her, something that made one feel…at home was the closest he could come to describing it.

'I understand from Minerva that your parents had a loving marriage,' she said.

If he did not wish to continue this conversation, now would be the time to acknowledge it and then suggest they go back to the house and dress for dinner.

'They were in love,' he said. 'After she died, my father was beyond consoling for a long time.'

'My parents were very much in love too.' The lively, curious expression in her lovely eyes dimmed. 'They died only a year ago, first Mother and the next day Father. They were unaware of each other's passing.'

'I am truly sorry to hear it, Evie.'

Perhaps it was this circumstance which had led to her becoming a companion. It did happen sometimes that women were not protected in such a situation.

If that was the case, she was safe here at Rivenhall. He would see to it.

And Minerva would be safe with a husband, once he could convince her to accept one.

'I imagine that my sister has also told you how happy my brother is with his wife?' He did not know why he brought that up, except that he wished to continue speaking with her.

William had been forced to wed his wife who, when they'd met, was a complete stranger.

Oddly enough, it was their example that he and Minerva each used to defend what a marriage ought to be. In his sister's opinion their marriage illustrated love being the reason to wed. But they had not been in love when they'd wed. William had married where his father appointed him to. His brother's choice to wed for the good of the family had ended in a happy marriage, which was Thomas's argument in it all.

While Thomas would also wed for the family's good, he did not hope to have what his brother had.

It was interesting that after a lifetime of disappointing Father, William had been the one to please him.

Thomas had spent his youth trying to please Father by learning to be the best heir he could be. From the age of twelve, he had devoted himself to it. After Mother's death he'd tried even harder, hoping to comfort Father.

William, as Thomas saw it, had devoted his time to pleasing Mother, who was a bright, joyful person who enjoyed a spot of mischief upon occasion. Father had adored her for it.

William and Mother were alike in looks and spirit. As a child Thomas had felt she loved his brother more. Because of it, he'd developed an attitude of competitiveness when it came to his brother.

Then the day had come when his mother came upon him unexpectedly while he was hiding in the conservatory. He had been torn between wanting to weep and wanting to get into a fight with William.

When he'd told her how he felt, she'd gathered him in her arms.

'It is true, your brother and I are alike in many ways and I love him.' She held him tight, kissing his hair while she spoke. 'But, Thomas, you must understand something. I love you no less because of it. You are like your father, so much like him, and you know that I adore your father. One day you will be Viscount and I hope you grow up to be exactly like him.'

That was the day he'd decided to please his mother by pleasing his father. He made every effort to one day be the Viscount his father was. Even though he believed what his mother told him, there had still been something driving him to be better than William. Better behaved, responsible and dependable. Above reproach in his behaviour.

He knew now how foolish it was.

For all his efforts, he'd quite recently discovered that Father did not love him any better for it. The fact that William had caused him no end of grief growing up did not change Father's love for him in the end.

Perhaps love could not be earned. Minerva was proof of it. His sister was turning Father's hair grey, displeasing him more than pleasing him, and yet he adored her.

Lost in his musings, he failed to see Evie stand. She was gazing down at him saying something. He had no idea what it was.

He caught a thread of it. Ah, she was talking about Lydia—that she had seen her shopping one day? It was something of the sort.

'I think she is a lovely and well-mannered lady, Thomas.'

'Oh…yes indeed.' He stood. 'And I am certain that if you and my sister discover anything to the contrary you will inform me of it.'

'Well, naturally, it is what sisters do, and friends as well.'

'May I conclude then that you count me as a friend, Evie?'

She smiled, glancing about for the kitten. 'I like you and Minerva both very well.' Since she had her back turned towards him he could not read her expression. 'And Rivenhall? It feels very much like home already.'

'Good then…and I like you, too, Evie.' She turned then and he did see her expression. Her smile, the sparkle in her eyes hit him in the heart…lodged deep. He could not imagine why, or what it meant. 'Minerva and I both do.'

His sister might like Evie as much as she pleased but the same was not true for him. Thomas could like her to a point, and not beyond. He would need to be careful not to let his feelings for Evie take an inappropriate turn.

She walked towards the darker part of the conservatory, looking this way and that.

'Where could she have got to?'

'Not far. I'll look to the left and you look to the right,' he suggested.

He walked, listened, walked and listened again. Ah, just there within the dense foliage of a large bush he heard rustling.

Kneeling, he reached into it. He gripped something… soft warm fur…and smooth warm fingers.

He leaned to the side to peer around the bush. At the same instant Evie poked her head around.

Pretty eyes, round and sparkling in the dim light, blinked at him. A joyful riot of red-blonde ringlets curled about her face.

All at once she smiled. 'Would you like to take her, Thomas?'

What? He had nearly forgotten there was a kitten between them. He had become distracted gazing into her eyes and breathless at the sensation of holding her hand. He had been unaware of anything else for a moment.

And then her fingers pulled out of his and he was holding the small cat. The kitten was warm, purring, and yet it was not nearly as warm as Evie's hand had been.

They stood. He held the kitten close to his heart since she went limp rather suddenly and fell asleep.

'Charm seems taken with you, Thomas.'

'I must admit, no one has ever fallen asleep in my arms before. Even William's twins wriggle and squirm until their mother rescues them.'

They both laughed over it, which felt good. Charm felt good in his hands, too, but it was the lingering touch of Evie's fingers on his mind.

He had danced with ladies at balls, spent time with them at tea, but he could honestly say that he had not enjoyed any of those times as well as he did walking from the conservatory, through the windy garden towards the house with Evie…his sister's friend.

And, he believed, his friend as well. All he needed to do was keep her that. Just a friend…not a friend who made his heart tip off-balance.

Chapter Six

Moments before the dinner party, Evie stood in front of the full-length mirror beside her wardrobe with Minerva looking over her shoulder.

'You look stunning.' Minerva nodded, her smile reflecting approval.

Evie did look pretty, but only because of the gown Minerva had loaned her. She missed the lovely garments she had been forced to leave behind and was grateful to be wearing this elegant and charming one.

It was soft amber with threads of shimmering bronze at the hem and sleeves. It was becoming and at the same time modest and not likely to stand out and attract attention.

Twirling about, she felt a bit like an autumn leaf drifting happily on a breeze.

She needed all the buoyant cheer she could gather about herself because the truth was, she was frightened. It was not as if all of society would be attending tonight, but it would only take one person from Gossmere who might recognise her and then she would be on the run again.

'Your maid did a skilful job of taming my hair,' Evie said. 'You should not have troubled her with it.'

Gazing in the mirror, she was reassured that she did not resemble her everyday self…and that Gossmere was a world away. The only ones to see her hair tamed into a lovely style would be people she did not yet know.

'Shall we go downstairs and see what we can learn of Lydia?' Minerva asked.

'But you know her already. You are neighbours after all.'

'Of course I know her, but not in the light of being future Viscountess Rivenhall.'

'I am certain she will suit your brother splendidly.'

'Truly?' Minerva asked while they descended the stairway. 'Why would you think so?'

As they walked, Evie was reminded of how different life here in London was. A gathering in Gossmere would not be nearly as elegant…as polished.

Even though it was October, large vases dripping with flowers lined the hallway leading to the large drawing room. She heard the strains of a pair of violins playing softly. Floors gleamed, reflecting the hem of her gown while they walked towards the festivities. For all that this was considered a causal dinner party, Evie felt that even Queen Victoria would feel comfortable here.

Closer to the drawing room she heard the soft hum of polite conversation filtering out of the open doorway.

'I suppose it is because your brother thinks so,' Evie said. 'If he believes she will suit, she probably will.'

'What he believes he needs is not what he needs.'

Pausing at the drawing room entrance, Minerva grasped her hand. 'For all that I give my brother grief, he is a wonderful man and I adore him. I simply cannot allow him to sacrifice himself to what he sees as his duty. If he cares for Lydia, and she cares for him, it is all well and good. But will you help me discover if they will suit?'

'I do not know what I can do. He will make his choice in the matter. Truly, Minerva, it is only right he should be allowed to do so. It is what I wish for myself and what you wish for yourself, is it not?'

'Yes, but we are correct and he is not.' Minerva shrugged. 'If you look over my shoulder you will see a lady in blue silk sitting in the chair beside the hearth— the red chair. She is Lydia.'

'She looks agreeable. She and your brother are speaking amicably to one another.'

'Is he smiling?'

'Well, no. But perhaps they are not discussing something light-hearted.'

'I can promise you, Thomas is not feeling light-hearted while speaking to her. A man ought to feel such a thing if he intends to court a lady, don't you think?' Yes, she did think so. Evie would not want to be courted by a man who did not feel happy to be doing it. 'Please, Evie, say you will help me to help my brother.'

'What can I do?'

'Just watch, see how the two of them are together and later tonight we shall meet and discuss what we find.'

'Yes. All right. I will do what I can.'

For what it was worth. Even if she and Minerva

came to the conclusion that Thomas and Miss Brownton would not make each other happy there was little they could do about it.

'Oh, thank you, Evie!' She gave her hands a quick squeeze. 'Onward we march.'

With that, she and Minerva entered the drawing room.

Glancing about, she scanned the crowd, fear crawling up her throat in anticipation of seeing a face from Gossmere.

All right, only strangers. Relief rushed through her. Her shoulders relaxed, her breathing evened out. She must learn to feel more confident in the company of visitors. They could hardly be avoided. Most days she and Minerva paid calls on her friends.

Really, the odds that she would encounter someone from home were remote.

She breathed a bit easier going about the room with Minerva, greeting people she had already met and some she had not.

Thomas, spotting them come into the room, joined them and helped to introduce her. Everyone was polite, welcoming her to London with genuine warmth. But still she kept close to Minerva and to Thomas because they were comfortable, familiar.

At one point Minerva left them to go across the room and chat with other friends. Evie had the oddest sensation that Thomas was somehow showing her off…to young gentlemen.

She could not imagine why. Were they not the very young men he wished his sister to notice? Did he imagine Minerva would be envious of the attention Evie was getting? Surely he would know better than that. But perhaps it was simply her own stress making her see events as odd.

After spending time with the young men, Thomas introduced her to Lydia Brownton, the lady who was the reason for the gathering, although she would not be aware of that.

Evie found her to be pleasant. A quiet, demure lady who was neither too loud nor too quiet. Too smiling or too grim. She was neutral—that was the impression Evie got of her. There was nothing wrong with that and perhaps Thomas liked it. For all she knew, he might be a man who enjoyed neutral to bright.

If so, he would not care for Evie's brighter looks. Not that it made a difference one way or another if he did, of course.

It seemed to her that if Thomas did marry Miss Brownton he would be able to go about his life without her presence making a ripple in his world...not a stir of angst. But just, perhaps, not a stir of delight either.

Glancing about, she wondered if any of the other ladies present might better suit him. They seemed interested enough, casting him smiles and seeming eager to be the one standing closest to him. Thomas was going to be Viscount one day and it was understandable that the ladies would wish to marry as well as they could. It was what their parents would have taught them, what society expected.

She glanced towards the ceiling. In her heart she looked all the way to Heaven, thanking her parents for showing her otherwise. Love was the most important thing.

After a while the company went in to dinner. She had been paired with an amicable young man who enjoyed talking on every subject.

Naturally she took advantage of the situation by discreetly enquiring about Lydia Brownton. Her dinner companion said that the lady was from an excellent family. Evie was certain Minerva would agree that this was not the stuff of a joyful marriage.

After the meal was finished Thomas broke with the tradition of men going to the library and ladies to the drawing room and invited everyone to gather back in the drawing room.

Perhaps there was a hint of rebellion in his soul. Of course, retiring to the drawing room did make sense since he was not seeking a future bride from among the gentlemen.

Honestly, there was nothing she could do to influence Thomas's decision in a bride. But she did consider him a friend and wished for him to be happy.

To that end she would sit quietly in her chair, observe his interactions with the ladies, particularly the neighbour, Lydia. Perhaps something would present itself.

It was a tricky thing, trying to get to know Lydia Brownton with so many people gathered in the drawing room. He could not appear to be favouring her. Gossip would explode.

James Murray was here, along with his wife and his cousin. Murray's cousin Elsa was a terrible gossip. Society had learned about William's antics because of that woman's wagging tongue—former antics that was.

The very last thing Thomas wanted was to be

talked about, to bring gossip once again to the door of Rivenhall.

As a proper host, he spent time with each person. Having done that, it was time to turn his attention to the person who was the reason for holding the dinner party. If he could not find a way to speak privately with Lydia there was no point to this gathering.

What he wished to do was walk in the garden with her. That, however, would be frowned upon—fodder for the gossip he wished to avoid. Gentlemen and ladies did not walk alone together.

Minerva must have sensed his dilemma because she made an announcement. 'Friends, I find it as stuffy as a wet blanket in here. Shall we stroll in the garden?'

That was an excellent suggestion since it would give him a chance to spend time with Lydia and yet be in the company of others.

A few of the group chose to go out, but more stayed inside where it was warm.

'Miss Brownton,' he said. 'Would you care to walk with me in the garden? It is beautiful this autumn evening.'

Evie, sitting close by, slid him a glance that he could not interpret. She was smiling and he did not know what to make of it except that she was encouraging him, even though he knew she did not approve of his motivation for marrying.

'I would, of course, but my parents are remaining inside, and I will not have a chaperone.'

What was he to do? He could not take her out alone. And she, being a proper lady, would refuse even if he offered.

'Minerva is walking with her friends so I am not occupied at the moment,' Evie said with a smile. How had he never noticed the subtle dimple in her chin? More, why was he noticing it now? 'I would be happy to go along as chaperone.'

Hopefully, when Evie said Minerva was walking with friends, there were gentlemen among them. He knew several who would welcome her attention if only she were willing to give it to them.

'Thank you, Miss Clarke.' That was one hurdle faced, now he simply needed to convince Lydia to brave the cool evening and walk with him. 'Would you be agreeable to taking the air, Miss Brownton? The fountain is lovely by moonlight.'

Oddly, Evie's smile faltered for half a second, but she recovered it so quickly he was left wondering if he had seen it happen at all.

'Yes, that would be pleasant,' Lydia answered.

Thomas motioned to the butler, who was standing beside the drawing room doorway, asking him to bring their coats.

Ten minutes later the three of them were taking in the crisp air, making their way towards the fountain. He and Lydia walked ahead of Evie, who trailed several yards behind.

As an experienced companion, she clearly knew how to give a couple privacy and proper company at the same time. He congratulated himself on making the wise choice of engaging her as companion to Minerva.

Thomas searched his mind for something to say to the lady beside him. The silence hanging between them was uncomfortable.

'Do you find autumn evenings pleasant, Miss Brownton?'

She nodded. Her hair was a light brown shade which did not glow in the torchlight they passed under. Having seen her many times, he knew what colour her hair was, but only now noted it did not shine. Although he could not fathom why it should matter in the least.

'Yes, I do.'

Now what to say?

'Do you have a favourite season?'

'Summer, of course. The same as everyone.'

Not everyone. Evie, he knew, greatly enjoyed the crisp air and bright colours of autumn. He glanced back briefly to see how far behind she was.

Not far, only passing under the last torch. Golden light reflected in her hair and made it glimmer.

He reminded himself that it was not essential that a Viscountess's hair glimmered. It was more important that she was skilled in social situations—excelled at running a household.

Lydia would have been trained to do so since she was a little girl.

'May I ask, what are your interests? Do you enjoy riding, perhaps?'

'Not riding, no. I am terrified of horses. But I do enjoy embroidery quite well. I am skilled at needlework.'

'That's...splendid,' he said, because it was something to fill up the silence that would have followed her remark. 'Do you enjoy the company of other animals? Is it only horses which scare you?'

Her voice was steady. Not a drone, exactly, but she did not have a great deal of inflection in her tone.

Funny how he had known her socially for years and never noticed that.

'Dogs do bite on occasion, you know. As for cats?' She hugged her coat tighter around her, appearing to give a shiver. 'They are rather mysterious creatures. And they scratch. I used to have a scar on my hand because of one. They also make people sneeze.'

He wondered if Evie could hear this conversation. She would greatly disagree with Lydia's opinion of cats. Coming to know Charm as he was, he thought he did too.

'And as for birds!' She quite clearly shivered in mentioning them. 'They screech in their cages, and the mess they make is perfectly nasty!'

Well, then, he could not continue the conversation by speaking of pets. There was embroidery, she did enjoy that. Naturally, he had even less interest in embroidery than Minerva did.

There must be something they had in common.

They walked a short distance and arrived at the fountain. He indicated they should sit.

Evie sat, too, but several discreet feet away. Oddly, he felt the companion's presence more intensely than the lady sitting closer to him. Had he been sitting beside Evie, conversation would flow easily, the moment would be comfortable, entertaining.

Probably it was due to the fact that he was not looking at Evie as a potential bride. The stakes were not as high.

But he was, in fact, looking at Evie. She was gazing up at the moon, seeming lost in delight at the sight.

He forced his attention back to Lydia, who had taken that very moment to glance at him. Caught out at catching his attention wandering, she gave her attention to her skirt, smoothed the gathers into neat rows.

Naturally, a tidy appearance would be all-important to a lady who wished to wed a future Viscount.

But did she wish it? It was difficult to tell. He only assumed she did since most ladies did wish to wed as well as they might.

Unless the lady wished to marry for love. His gaze slid sideways again. Quick as a wayward thought, he snapped it back.

Miss Lydia Brownton might not sparkle, but there was nothing dislikeable about her. She was perfectly appropriate for his needs in a wife.

If she were not, his father would not have urged him to court her.

It was nearly midnight when Minerva left Evie's chamber. They had spent two hours chatting in their nightgowns and eating leftover apple cakes from dessert. It had not been only Thomas and Lydia they'd discussed, but the pair had been the focus of their attention.

Life as Minerva's friend was delightful. They got along famously. She'd slipped into the place Mary had been as naturally as birds twittered in trees.

Evie went to the doors, stepping out onto the small balcony. The air was cool, fresh and so much more delightful than it had been earlier in the day. A breeze had come up and blown out the smoke that tended to press upon the city.

London did have its charm, truly she enjoyed living here…but she did miss home, where the air was always clean and easy to breathe.

She put the thought away in favour of gazing down at the pretty garden below. She would embrace this lovely place since she was not likely to see the landscapes of Gossmere again.

A movement below caught her eye.

Seeing who it was, she smiled. Thomas walked in the garden. His figure was only illuminated by moonlight since the torches had been extinguished for the night.

Hmm…if she was in Gossmere she would not be seeing him strolling among the rows and hedges.

Even in the dim light she could tell he was deep in thought. His hands were shoved in his pockets and his head hung low. Perhaps he was thinking about the time he'd spent with Lydia Brownton earlier tonight.

What had he concluded about her? she could not help but wonder. Probably not what she and Minerva had concluded.

After reporting to Minerva what she had seen and heard tonight—that Lydia disliked riding, animals, and was not best pleased with autumn weather—they'd both concluded that Thomas would not be happy in the match. Truly, how could he find enjoyment in watching her stitch the Rivenhall name on handkerchiefs? How dreary.

Minerva proposed that they ought to do something to thwart the match. Evie did not think so. She held fast to her point that if they themselves wished a choice in marriage, Thomas ought to be afforded the same. Which did not mean she did not hope he chose elsewhere.

While she watched, he turned and came back into the house.

In spite of her view that he was free to choose a bride without her and Minerva's interference, she had half a mind to run downstairs and warn him that his choice was wrong. That he ought to look for another lady.

Not Evie, naturally. She was his sister's companion, a friend of the family. And she did keep a rather important secret from both of them.

She had to remind herself that there was only a small chance of being found out. It was rare for the Haverly household to come to London. Also, London was a very large city...although she would feel more at ease if Thomas was not acquainted with Mary's father.

All things considered, she was safer than Thomas was. At least in terms of making the correct decision for his life.

Yet again she was gripped by the urge to run downstairs and tell him he was making a mistake. But she was in her nightgown and could not possibly do so. Besides, he had probably come up to his chamber already.

Her mind stalled, lingering on the image of her sailing boldly into his chamber, or sneaking slowly into it wearing the perfectly respectable nightgown—all right, in her imagination it was not at all respectable.

'Oh, my stars!' she exclaimed. Why on earth had something like that invaded her mind? No doubt at this very moment Thomas was thinking about Lydia Brownton. Was he thinking of the lacking charms of the lady?

What an uncharitable thing to imagine. What was wrong with her?

She could not possibly be jealous since…well, since she was not in a position to be. But she was in a position to be supportive, no matter where he gave his heart.

But that was not right. He had no intention of giving his heart. Which, in her estimation, was not right either.

All of a sudden the wind rose, whipping the hem of her gown about her ankles. Chilly air twirled up her legs, so she went inside. She closed the doors, leaning back against them.

She sighed soul deep…because not only was Thomas not going to give his heart, he was not going to give it to her.

If that had been jealousy she'd felt a moment ago, it was vastly misplaced. A fellow needed to be one's own in order to feel envious of his attentions.

Thomas Grant was not her own and never would be.

Crossing the room, she fell backwards on the bed, covering her eyes with her arm. Better to turn her attention to the other matters she and Minerva had been discussing.

One of them had been her friend's new 'cause', which Evie had declined to discuss with Thomas. For one thing it was not for her to reveal his sister's business, and for another it was a worthy cause and if he knew of it he would likely forbid it.

What she and Minerva both considered a crime was the way animals all over London were being sold, and kept in inhumane conditions. Especially exotic animals, who were never meant to be pets, regardless of how much money someone was willing to pay for them.

Jamrach's Wild Beast Emporium was a disgrace to civilised society, but there were other shops even worse than that. And yet civilised society seemed to enjoy possessing beasts who were meant to roam free.

The animals were impressive to be sure and a thrill to see, but that did not mean it was right to keep them. No doubt the sad-looking elephant at the circus had been purchased from a shop such as Jamrach's.

Evie had no idea what she and Minerva were to do about the injustice any more than she knew what they ought to do about Thomas throwing his happiness away.

Once again her mind turned to the place she had tried to steer it away from by thinking of captive beasts. Why was it that her thoughts tended to return to Thomas time after time? It was beyond her why they should do so.

The only thing to do in the moment was to go to sleep and put it from her mind.

Oh, dear, her mind had other ideas. A vision of Thomas's face lingered quite against her will…perhaps not against her will, if she were to be honest.

Fascinated by her vision, she watched him frown. His brows lowered over mesmerising eyes. Next she watched his smile. Now his brows lifted, his gaze peered at her in what could only be humour. A stray strand of hair crossed his forehead. She caught the bare suggestion of a dimple at the corner of his mouth.

Was that something she had seen or was she imagining it because she enjoyed dimples?

She drifted slowly to sleep wondering about it.

Chapter Seven

'Here we are!' Minerva declared when the carriage driver stopped in front of Millie's Tea House.

Thomas hid a sigh. For some reason his sister wanted desperately to come here, even though they might have had a nice tea at home.

The driver opened the door, helping the ladies down the steps.

'What a charming place,' Evie said.

There were shops on the same road. The windows were crowded with trinkets and fripperies which a lady might enjoy. Several doors down was one of the exotic pet stores so popular in London these days. Even from here he could hear a parrot screeching.

No sooner had they taken a table near a lace-curtained window than Minerva popped up from her chair.

'I saw a pair of gloves in the window next door. I am going to purchase them.'

'Can it wait until after tea?' Thomas asked. 'We only just sat down.'

'If I could be certain that no one else would buy them while I was in here, then yes. But they are the sweetest things I have ever seen and so I shall go now.'

Evie began to rise, but Minerva gestured for her to remain seated.

'I'll only be a moment. Please keep my brother company since he was good enough to come with us.'

His sister was up to something, although what it could be he could not imagine. But just because he could not imagine it did not mean he could not feel it in his bones.

'Order me a scone, Thomas,' she said before hurrying out of the door.

'Your sister tells me they are quite delicious,' Evie commented, glancing about the small bakery.

It was charming, quite feminine in decor. Curtains of ivory lace hung at every window and the same lace-covered tables were scattered about the room. A cheerful fire snapped in the small corner hearth, which was welcome. This time of year, the afternoons were turning chilly.

They were the only customers at the moment. A round, cheerful-looking woman came out of a back room, wiping her hands on an apron made of lace tied about her middle. It was the same lace which was draped across the windows and covered the tables.

She took their order and then bustled back the way she had come, to the kitchen, he imagined, since delicious scents wafted into the dining room when she opened the door.

'It was kind of you to accompany us,' Evie said.

'Not as kind as you might think. I've been attending to Rivenhall business all day. I needed an outing.'

Yellow and gold leaves blew past the window. Evie smiled at them. 'It is far too pleasant a day to be stuck inside.'

More than the day, the company was pleasant.

'I hope you enjoyed the dinner party the other night.' More than he had.

Instantly, he regretted the unkind thought.

If he had not enjoyed the evening it was his own fault. His intention had been to spend time with Lydia Brownton and he had done that. It was hardly Lydia's fault that his attention had kept wandering to the lady who had been their chaperone.

In the future he would make sure his focus remained where it belonged. It had been difficult to appreciate Lydia's demure spirit when it was overshadowed by Evie's bright one. It was a quality he had long admired.

'I had a marvellous time, Thomas. Your friends were so welcoming to me.'

'I did notice that.' How could he not? 'Especially the young men. They seemed taken with you, Evie.'

A situation which had pleased him and, at the same time, oddly annoyed him.

'Only because a new face in the group is always diverting.'

That was true. Especially when the new face had such a becoming smile and little curls constantly breaking the restraint of her hairstyle. That would command any man's attention.

If he, a man who was not looking at his sister's companion with courting on his mind, noticed how compelling she was, it was safe to assume that several young dandies leaving the gathering had been smitten with her.

'And how was your evening? I noticed that you spent a great deal of time with Miss Brownton after we came back inside.'

'I wonder if others noticed,' he murmured without thinking. For some reason it seemed easy to speak his mind when he was with Evie.

'Would it be so awful if they did? Surely they expect you to select a lady to court at some point.'

'I need to, of course. It is my duty, my obligation to Rivenhall.'

'But is it what you wish, Thomas? Surely obligation is not enough to build your marriage on. What you want should count more than that.'

The woman with the lace apron returned, carrying a tray with three cups of tea and a selection of scones. With a nod and a smile she went back to her kitchen.

'If you want to know the truth...' He paused, wondering if he was really going to speak it.

'My belief is that there is no point in speaking if it is not the truth,' Evie said, curling her hand and then resting her chin on it.

Once again he congratulated himself on engaging such an honest and sensible companion for Minerva.

'I have known all my life that I must marry for a different reason than some men. As future Viscount I have different things to consider in a wife.'

Evie frowned. She huffed out a small puff of breath which made her opinion known more forcefully than words.

'Clearly, you do not agree. But since we are speaking honestly, I will tell you something—to you it may sound harsh, but it is my reality. If I wed a woman that society does not approve of, there will be talk.'

'Oh, but, Thomas, who cares if they talk? Isn't your happiness more important than what people have to say?'

'I care. My brother caused too much talk over the years. Ever since we were boys he was up to mischief. I will not cause my father shame, especially now, when he is ill.'

'And you did not get into mischief? You were a boy at one time. It is what they do, I understand.'

He could not get over how easy it was being with Evie. Why was that? He could not recall ever meeting anyone he connected with so naturally. Nor as quickly.

Minerva was taking her time coming back and he found he didn't mind all that much. At least he would not if he did not still have the sense she was not actually purchasing the loveliest gloves she had ever seen.

'I did, yes, but there came a time when I learned what was expected of me as heir.'

Chin still propped in her palm, she tapped her fingers on her cheek. Her brows dipped in a frown, subtly dimming the blue-green shade of her eyes.

'You do not approve of my reasoning,' he said.

She shook her head.

'You should not have given up your childhood, in my opinion.'

'It is different for the heir to a Viscount. But what about young girls, Evie? Do they also run around and get into mischief…? But then, I know they do, don't I? I suppose what I am asking is if you did.'

'Yes,' she said quietly, her demeanour subdued. He could not imagine what he had said to make her look sad.

'Did I say something out of line? I apologise if I did.'

'No, Thomas, you did not. It is only that it has been but a year since I lost my parents. Thinking of my childhood, which was quite happy, reminds me of the loss all over again.'

'I understand how you feel. I wish I could tell you it gets easier.'

'I wish it too.'

Reaching across the table, he clasped her hand, squeezing her slender fingers. Grief did not get easier, but sharing it helped.

Minerva swept into the shop, along with a gust of cool wind. Suddenly realising they were in public, he pulled his hand away. He ought to have let go of Evie's hand a second earlier. Minerva was bound to misinterpret his reason for touching her companion.

The only comment she made was a silent one— lifting her brows, biting back a smile. He would set her straight on the matter, but there was little point. His sister would see the mischief in the situation, no matter what he had to say about it.

'It is getting cloudy and, oh, so cold! But you should see the shop, Evie. It is extraordinary, so many exotic items to purchase. Why, the slippers from, well, I do not know from where, but the colours alone are enough to make a lady open her purse.'

He had not seen brightly hued slippers in the window when they'd passed by, but clearly that was where she had gone since she was showing off her new gloves to Evie with great pleasure.

To him they looked like ordinary gloves, but he was not an expert in what ladies admired.

He dismissed the gloves from his mind in favour of enjoying pleasant company over tea.

It was raining. Ever since the clouds had rolled in during tea at Millie's yesterday afternoon it had not stopped, not even for a moment. To Evie's way of thinking, rain was as wonderful as leaves being driven along by brisk wind.

Changeable weather was simply exciting. It was not as if being kept indoors left her with nothing to do. She had spent the day exploring the house. From attic to kitchen she found it to be a charming place to live. It would be a sad day for Evie when she had to leave here. One day Minerva would marry—perhaps she would, at any rate.

With Minerva's situation changed, Evie's would also be. One thing would not change. Their friendship. That would continue even if she were not receiving an allowance for it.

She might also lose her position if Thomas got wind of what she and Minerva were planning. She had apologised for getting his sister into trouble at the circus and meant it whole-heartedly. And now, well, something else had come up which called for secrecy…stealth and a bold heart.

This time the scheme had been devised by Minerva. It was a good one, to be sure, and she was going to go along with it. What they had in mind would need to wait until the weather cleared, but it could not be put off too long.

Thomas had not waited for the weather to clear before going on his errand. He had braved the elements, gone next door to have tea with Lydia Brownton.

In her opinion such an outing should not be considered an errand, but she feared that was how he saw it. This visit was a very big first step for him and one she hoped he would not in the end regret. If she were a matchmaker she would never put the two of them together.

Oh, my stars, that was an uncharitable thought.

This was a perfect afternoon to sit by a window and read, so she left her chamber and went to the library. Along the way she determined to be kinder in her opinions.

'I hope he is having a marvellous time,' she murmured, entering the library.

What a grand room this was, with tall windows along one wall and bookcases nearly to the ceiling. There was a ladder to reach the books on the lower level, but for the books higher up there were stairs leading to a catwalk.

A large fireplace with crackling flames warmed the room. Two couches and several chairs invited one to sit and relax. Which she intended to do. What could be nicer than a good book and a comfortable chair beside a window on a stormy day?

Only three pages into the story, she discovered what could be nicer.

The door opened and Thomas entered. He did not see her at first because he was industriously shaking raindrops from his hair. She wondered if Lydia appreci-

ated how handsome he was. But of course she would—
it was clear for anyone to see.

With a sigh, she reminded herself that it was not her
place to wonder such a thing. Unless she was wondering it with complete objectivity. That would be acceptable. One could observe handsomeness without having
one's heart react to it.

At the dinner party there had been several men
whom she believed had been invited to attract Minerva's attention. She did not think her friend's heart had
reacted to any of those handsome faces.

Evie's heart had not fluttered over them either. Not
like it was doing right now. Chances were it had something to do with Thomas shaking the raindrops from
his hair and she enjoyed a good storm.

'Oh, hello, Evie.'

'Good afternoon, Thomas.'

Her pattering heart was only affected by the way the
autumn weather clung to him because, really, he was
not at all her type. When she gave her heart to a man it
would be to one who was constantly cheerful. She had
always dreamed of loving a man with a quick smile and
a cheerful disposition.

Thomas Grant was not that man. He was a man with
his mind set on courting his neighbour.

She was a woman who would force her heart to re-
gain its normal rhythm.

She closed the book and stood. 'I will leave you to
your library, Thomas.'

'Won't you stay? There is room for both of us. I
would not wish to drive you away.'

She sat down again, but did not open the book.

'Did you enjoy tea with Miss Lydia?' she asked, because when it came down to it, true life was more interesting than a story. And she was interested in knowing if he'd had a good time. Truly, she did hope for his happiness.

Friends always wished that for each other.

'It was tea…' He shrugged.

'But did you enjoy it?'

'Yes, naturally.' He went to the window, gazing out. 'The cucumber sandwiches were quite good.'

It was telling that he had not first mentioned the pleasant company of a suitable lady.

'I trust Miss Lydia is well on this rainy afternoon?'

'She seemed so. But I do not believe she favours the rain.' It was interesting that he frowned when he spoke of her. But he tended to frown so perhaps it did not mean anything.

'I imagine people will now guess that you intend to court her, since you paid her a call.'

If she could take back the words she would. My stars! For an issue that was not her business, she dwelt upon it rather frequently. She feared he would think her too curious about him.

'A future Viscount's business seems to be everyone's business and it does get remarked upon,' he said.

'Your behaviour is above gossip. You go to great lengths to make sure of it.'

'After what we went through with William's past behaviour and Minerva's stunts… Well, I wish to avoid it as much as possible. But, given who I am, there is not much to be done about it.'

Oh, dear… She and Minerva were about to do something—not a stunt, of course. It was much more important than that. Still, if Thomas got wind of it he would be quite unhappy.

'Once you announce your engagement, I imagine the talk will subside. Besides, it is merely delightful speculation, not true gossip. Miss Lydia is a proper lady and you are a proper gentleman. Really, what untoward thing can be said of the two of you?'

Not a single thing in her opinion, since, from what she could tell, there had been no spark whatsoever. It seemed to her that during the time they'd spent together in the garden he had struggled to even find something to converse with her about.

If Evie did not like him so well she would leave him to choose a cheerless life. For all she knew, he might want a joyless life.

That was nonsense. No one wanted that! It was time for him to do something joyful. Just so that he would understand what he would be giving up in the marriage he envisaged.

Setting the book aside, she rose and joined him at the window.

'Do you enjoy the rain, Thomas?'

'I do enjoy it.' He nodded.

'What do you say we go outside and splash about for a few moments?'

'Now, do you mean?'

She caught his hand and tugged on it. Oh, she should not have done that, but he did have a wonderful long-fingered hand and she liked the way it felt so strong and warm.

'Yes, now...before the rain stops!'

Thomas jumped in a beautifully deep puddle.

Evie dodged the spray, letting out a funny screeching laugh.

'Watch out, Thomas Grant!' she cried, sweeping her foot sideways and creating a wave, and he was not quick enough to leap out of the way. His trouser legs got gloriously soaked.

He ought to care that he had only recently dried out from rushing home from next door, but oddly, he did not.

When he'd told Evie he enjoyed the rain he'd meant more that he enjoyed watching it from a warm, dry place. But the call to fun dancing in her eyes, the tug of her small, soft hand had been compelling. He could not resist the merry time she offered.

That was not quite true. He could have resisted if he'd tried a little harder. He had resisted merry times far more than he had indulged in them so it ought to have been a simple thing.

Evie turned her face up to the rain, arms spread wide while turning in a slow circle. He found himself simply standing and staring.

There was nothing simple about resisting Evie Clarke so there was no point in trying.

If he danced light-heartedly within the walls of his own garden, there would be no one to see and report to society.

'Miss Clarke?' He presented a playful half bow and

then extended his hand. 'Will you do me the honour of a puddle dance?'

'A puddle dance! Whatever that is, it sounds wonderful.' She placed her fingers in his palm.

He touched her waist and she put her other hand on his shoulder. Humming a tune, he whirled her towards a nearly pond-sized puddle.

'Now what?' she asked.

Her hair, thoroughly damp, was a riot of curls, her eyes sparkled in clear delight. Evie Clarke was utterly enchanting.

'The steps are simple. Holding our pose, we stamp and splash and see who gets the wettest.'

'Thomas, my friend, you cannot tell me you are not as mischievous as your brother and sister.'

He winked.

She laughed.

All of a sudden he was reminded of how his mother used to smile at whatever trouble he and William found to get into.

But this was now, and it was Evie smiling. They stamped, leapt and splashed and all the while held the proper dance pose.

And they laughed until their sides ached.

He should laugh more often, perhaps. And yet he knew that once they left the garden and resumed normal life he would once again be the sober-minded man he had grown to be. It would be so whether he wished to be or not. It was required of the role he would inherit.

'Well, then, that was great fun,' she said breathlessly. 'Thank you for teaching me.'

'I forgot how much fun it was.' Seeing her flushed cheeks and her quick breathing, he was breathless too.

'You've done this before? I thought you might have made it up just now.'

'William and I used to do something like it…just… well, we were not holding each other when we did.'

'It is a grand dance. I only wish it was not getting cold, but I fear we should go back inside.'

'Shall we do it again next time it rains?' What had got into him? This was a moment out of time which he would not be repeating.

'You should teach Lydia the puddle dance.'

'She does not appreciate rain.'

Evie pursed her lips as if she had something to say, but did not say it.

'What are you thinking?'

'It is not my place to think anything.' She was beginning to shiver. For as much as he would like to hold her close and keep her warm while they walked back to the house, it would be inappropriate.

'And yet you do.'

She folded her arms across her chest, curling her hands and tucking them in for warmth.

'I believe in a husband and wife sharing interests. I believe that marriage should be fun. Full of laughter.'

'And I believe that marriage fulfils social obligation…is meant for the betterment of society.'

'It is a lucky thing we are not marrying each other, then,' she answered.

She smiled when she said it so he did not take it to heart.

'Indeed a lucky thing.'

For as much as he liked her and enjoyed her company, what they saw for their futures was not at all the same. To risk offering his heart, as she was willing to do, was simply beyond him.

His heart did not beat in triple time for his neighbour and was therefore perfectly safe.

Chapter Eight

Attending the theatre was not Thomas's first choice of how to spend an evening, but Minerva and Evie had their hearts set on seeing tonight's performance. It was reported to be a dull programme and he could not imagine why the ladies were so determined to attend.

Unless it was connected with whatever mischief he suspected they were planning.

'I do not know who you are, Thomas.' Minerva blinked up at him while they waited in the foyer for the carriage to be brought around and for Evie to come downstairs.

'What have I done now?'

'Danced in the rain! I would not have believed it to be you had Evie not assured me it was.'

He prickled a bit that Evie had discussed it. Felt somehow that a secret part of himself had been exposed. Not that it was a secret to his sister, but still. He did not appreciate a private moment being discussed.

'I heard you laughing and looked out of the window. And I feel the need to point out that having fun is not a character flaw to be kept secret. So you need not look so sour.'

'If I am sour it is only that you are dragging me to the theatre to watch a performance which everyone says is tedious at best.'

'Evie and I can go on our own if you like.'

No, they could not. Those two were up to something and he was not about to leave them to it.

'But back to the subject at hand. You would not have had such a grand time dancing in the rain with Lydia.'

'When was that the subject at hand?' And he had no way of knowing if it was true or not since his neighbour would not have ventured out in the rain.

'If it was not, it ought to have been. You are a fabulous brother, Thomas, and you should allow yourself a spot of merriment. Here comes Evie now.'

Minerva rushed across the foyer. The ladies spoke quietly for a moment. Secretively, to put a finer point on it.

Evie glanced over at him with a frown while his sister grinned. That was curious. He would need to be on his guard tonight. Whatever they were up to, he meant to prevent it.

Mischief was not the only thing he needed to guard against tonight. He was thinking of Evie far too often.

That tendency was not good for him. All it did was confuse him. A moment of fun with a friend was all well and good, but it was his future he needed to keep uppermost in his mind.

That future lay with the very appropriate Lydia, not with fun and pretty Evie.

Feeling anything beyond friendship for his sister's

companion would open the door to heartache. What they each required of a marriage did not agree. At least he and Lydia were of like mind on it.

He assumed they were at any rate, although he had yet to bring up the subject of marriage with her. But Lydia had been raised to be the wife of a peer, which could only mean they understood each other in what was required of a society marriage.

On a deep sigh, he pursed his lips and then firmed them.

He was never going to dance in the rain again.

What a relief it was to finally reach the intermission of the show. It really was as boring as everyone claimed it was. But she and Minerva had chosen this show because the playhouse was only a few doors down from where the captive parrots were kept—at least they were when Minerva had slipped away from tea at Millie's to explore the exotic animal shop.

The cold night air in the alley behind the theatre was brisk and wonderful. Evie could barely get enough into her lungs to expel the stuffy atmosphere inside, where a dozen cloying perfumes competed with one another.

'We cannot be sure the parrots are still being kept under the awning behind the shop. They may have been moved inside.'

'Perhaps they have. If so, we will simply have to break in to free them.' Minerva did not seem to have any hesitation at the prospect of doing so.

'We will not have enough time. Your brother will wonder why we are taking so long to visit the ladies' room,' she pointed out.

'It is true. I know he is suspicious of us as it is. Still, it is our only chance to get this done.'

'And we have used the excuse before,' Evie whispered, glancing over her shoulder while they rushed down the alley.

Some alleys in the city were terribly dangerous, but Minerva assured her this was a quiet one. The only thieves and miscreants were likely to be the two of them.

'Do you hear the birds?' Evie did. The sound was faint at this distance, but they were putting up an awful squawk, as if a predator was threatening their cage.

'Oh, the poor things. The wonder is that they have any room to raise a fuss, the way they are packed together like sardines in a tin. We should hurry.'

And so they picked up their skirts and ran.

Minerva had not exaggerated the conditions the poor birds were kept in. If there was a crime here, it was by the hand of the captors, not the liberators.

Indeed, the men who had stolen the exotic green creatures from their home in the Amazon were the true thieves. The birds were nothing less than living jewels and ought to have been cherished as such, not crammed together like inert merchandise.

She and Minerva were the heroes of the evening. At least they would be if they could complete the liberation before Thomas discovered what they were up to.

The cause for the parrots' distress, a pair of stray dogs looking for an easy meal, dashed away when Minerva waved her arms and shouted at them.

Evie wished she had only waved her arms because her shout was rather loud and anyone might have heard it. If they were caught, she hated to think how Thomas would react.

This misadventure was far worse than sneaking away to visit circus performers. Stealing had legal consequences. She and Minerva could end up shamed, incarcerated. Thomas's worst nightmare would come true. Minerva's marriage prospects might become greatly hindered.

'I think we should go back now,' she suggested.

'I cannot.' Minerva shook her head. 'But I do not hold you to this.'

Standing beside the cage of now listless birds, she knew there really was no choice but to carry on.

Evie thought it quite odd that the birds were treated so wickedly, considering the sellers stood to make a great deal of money from their sale. Perhaps to them losing one or two of them was the cost of doing business. To her it was unconscionable, not to be borne a second longer.

'I do not know why they could not have brought them inside and cared for them,' she stated.

'Because they are brutes!'

'Of the worst order.'

'But are we doing the right thing?'

A pair of hands came down, one on her shoulder and one on Minerva's.

'That is a very good question.'

'Thomas! You came just in time,' Minerva said, sounding quite calm, as if they had been expecting him all along and he had arrived late. She spun out from under his hand. Evie remained where she was, feeling rather frozen. 'We might have got a splinter if we tried to pry off the lid to save the birds.'

'Steal the birds, you mean. I will not allow it.'

'We are not stealing them.' Evie declared, shaking Thomas's hand off her shoulder. 'Minerva just wanted me to see the conditions the birds are being kept in so we can try to help them.'

'Whatever you are doing, I forbid it.'

Minerva laughed, grabbed a slat and yanked it. As a result, the top of the crate loosened and she tossed it aside.

'I do not know my own strength.'

Evie gasped. 'Minerva, no! You can't do that…'

A beautiful bird used its beak to climb to the top. It climbed back down the outside of the crate. Standing on the pavement, it cocked its head, one curious eye flashing at them.

'You see, Thomas,' Minerva said, 'it is thanking us.'

'Why isn't it flying?' Thomas asked. 'Quick, put it back inside.' He picked it up when neither of them moved. It promptly bit his thumb and held on.

The other birds took courage seeing their fellow captive's victory and climbed out after it. Within a moment the pavement behind the shop was dotted with waddling parrots all screeching at once.

Thomas hopped about among the birds on the ground. She had to admire that even in his distress he was careful not to step on any of them.

She was not certain she had ever seen anything so funny. Oh, my word, the sight of him silently hopping was beyond price.

'Hold still! Let me prise it off you,' Evie said.

Or tried to say, but she was gasping with laughter because how could anyone not be? She had never seen anything like this and would not see it again.

A man dancing about with a parrot hanging from his thumb and a dozen others waddling underfoot was a sight to behold.

Although it was funny, it was time to rescue Thomas from his predicament. She touched the bird's wing. It let go of Thomas and reached its beak towards her. Thomas took the instant to grab the bird and toss it up.

It flapped clumsily over their heads and then managed to land in a nearby tree.

'I think their wings have grown weak and it is difficult for them to fly,' Thomas declared. 'Quick, give them a toss and see if they can manage. But be careful!'

He shook his thumb then sucked on the spot where the sharp beak had left a welt on his skin.

Grabbing the bird closest to his foot, he hefted it up. They all gazed up, watching it beat the air and then make it to the tree and then wrap its claws around a branch.

To her utter amazement, a great wide grin replaced Thomas's frown. 'We just did this, didn't we? We broke the law in the cause of justice,' he said.

Bending, she scooped up a bird and tossed it up. It followed its fellows into the tree.

'Let's get the rest of them up there before someone comes out of the store and catches them again...and us,' he said.

'Oh, dear—one of them just toddled off down the alley!' Minerva exclaimed. 'I'll go and get it!'

Something else thrilling had happened. Thomas,

their foe, had become their ally…and he was laughing over the adventure.

In short order the rest of the birds were clumsily making their way to the sanctuary of the tree branches. This time of year, there were very few leaves left on the tree and so the birds were not hidden, but they were safe from wandering dogs at least.

Side by side, she and Thomas gazed up at them. She knew he was as pleased as she was that the birds were free—and, so far, they had not been caught out as criminals.

'I am so proud of you, Thomas!' She was. Even though he was not hers to be proud of. Even though in the beginning it had been his intention to forbid them.

What mattered was that he had come around in the end and helped them. Indeed, it mattered very much.

'I am pleased to be your friend, Thomas.' She touched his arm in the friendliest of gestures.

'I'm pleased to know you, too, Evie.' He touched her fingers, patted them, also in the friendliest of gestures.

And then…and then her heart caught in her throat, squeezed tight. The look shining in his eyes could not be mistaken as friendly. Oh, but surely she was mistaken in what it was.

Or she was not.

'You…um…' She stumbled for something to say because he was staring at her mouth. 'You were so brave in the face of being assaulted by a fierce bird.'

His head went to one side ever so slightly, then he took her hand from his arm and pressed it to his heart. His handsome mouth quirked up at one corner.

'Evie…this one night… I do not believe it is meant

for following rules.' Using the hand not pressing her palm to his heart...his rapidly pounding heart...he touched her shoulder, drew her closer.

'An unusual evening. Quite out of the normal,' she whispered back. Whispered because where was her voice?

Snatched away in his simmering gaze was where.

She had never seen that sort of look directed at her before and she felt quite overcome by the sensation, of what it meant.

He wanted to kiss her, was trying not to, she knew that much...but he was going to do it anyway.

And she wanted to kiss him, was trying not to...but she was going to do it anyway. Oh, yes, indeed, she was.

This was but one moment out of time. Just because her life was going one way and his was going another did not mean that for this brief instant they could not...

Oh, but then his lips came gently down upon her mouth, lingered and...and what would really be so awful if their paths did somehow align?

So close, she felt his warmth intimately. She pressed closer, giving her own heat back to him. His arm, circled around her back, hinted at his strength.

Hinted at what could be between them if only...but there was no if only...just this moment out of time.

They had agreed this was all there was to it.

She pushed away, touched his cheek, wondering if he was thinking the same—regretted this was all there would be. Did his heart swell and make him feel like weeping?

Treading water, ready to sink to a place she had never

been, she reminded herself that Thomas was her friend. Grasped the reality and held on.

What a fool she had been to think she could kiss a friend, smile and forget it. This friend was about to court a woman, a safe woman whom his father approved of and one he need not risk his heart with.

What she needed was a man who would take that risk, freely offer his heart in love.

What a mistake she had made!

A horrid and lovely mistake.

Hearing Minerva's footsteps tapping up the alley, Thomas stepped away from Evie, the spell that wrapped them in a brief moment of magic broken as neatly as if it had been dumped in the Thames.

He shoved his hands behind his back, rocked on his heels and tried to whistle a casual tune, but it caught behind his teeth. He wondered why he even tried to make his sister believe nothing had happened while she was away. She was far too perceptive. He might as well have kissed Evie right in front of her.

As blunders went, he had committed a large one. Two, really.

Caught between watching the blush fade from Evie's cheeks, and yes, he could see it even in the dim light, and listening to the birds squawking in the tree, he wondered which mistake was the biggest.

Setting the birds free could see them ending up at the constable's office if they did not get away from here immediately.

But kissing Evie? Oh, it had been wonderful…the most thrilling kiss of his life, truth be told.

Also, truth be told, he hadn't a great many kisses in his past, not like the dozens that William did.

But, in the end, he should not have done it.

He had always been so careful not to risk being caught in a compromising situation. Rivenhall depended upon him making a wise, studied choice in a bride. Certainly not one based upon a heat-of-the-moment emotion.

What had come over him, kissing a woman in the open where anyone might see?

Very well, it was not what had come over him—but who.

Evie Clarke.

To try and clear the confusion, he thought about his responsibility as future Viscount. He thought of his father being ill and how he needed to do his duty and wed Lydia, the lady his father favoured.

He tried to summon an image of proper and demure Lydia, but with Evie's heat still lingering in his arms he could not quite manage it.

Imagining his father's favour rallied him, steadied him. With reason returning, he reminded himself that Evie was never meant to be his. In reality, in a short time a handsome young man was bound to sweep Evie off her feet with the declaration of true love she so longed for.

Very soon she would have what she wanted and he would have what he…wanted?

But yes, of course what he wanted…what he had set his mind to.

If he was haunted by the feel of Evie's sweet, giving body pressed against his heart, he would simply resign it to the delightful memory of one night and nothing more. Echoes were echoes, were they not? Heard and then forgotten.

Then a door slammed, landing him face to face with the consequences of the night's deed.

An outraged-looking fellow marched down the back steps of the shop. But, as bad as the situation was, in a small way Thomas did not regret freeing the birds. Only the consequences of it.

In freeing them, something within himself had been freed. Or rediscovered perhaps. He had been a carefree child once and for those few moments of mischief he'd felt that child stir.

What he did regret was any repercussions which might affect Minerva's future—and what his father would have to say about the incident.

'What is the meaning of this?' Thomas was not certain he had ever seen anyone so red-in-the-jowls angry. The man would be losing a pretty penny so in a sense Thomas understood how he must feel.

'I accept responsibility for it.' He stood tall, summoning the attitude his father would take with the man. 'Ladies, you may go home while I deal with the shopkeeper.'

'And that you will! Each and every one of you.'

'Oh, but sir!' Minerva splayed her fingers on her cheeks in an expression of contrition. She approached the shopkeeper.

Thomas stepped between them, but she swerved around him. What the blazes was she up to now?

'May I have a word before you have my brother arrested?'

'Be quick about it,' he grumbled.

'I would like to say how very sorry I am about the parrots. They are simply exquisite creatures and I understand what a loss they must be to you.'

Thomas heard Evie's quiet snort when she moved closer to him.

'Indeed, young woman, a great loss, which shall be answered for.'

'As it should be…but this was all a great accident for all it appears intentional. You see, my father, Lord Rivenhall, is on an extended holiday in Scotland and, to be honest, I may be honest with you, I hope?'

The fellow blinked, seeming confused, then nodded.

'The truth is, I have been desperately lonely, nearly undone by missing him. Naturally, I was certain a parrot would help.' She pointed to the tree. 'That one up there—the green one with the sad expression in its eyes. But when my brother Thomas and I came to purchase him, your excellent establishment was already closed. I cried for hours until Thomas feared for my health. So we came here to take my bird and then we intended to come back in the morning and pay whatever price you asked. Truly, he is the best of brothers and no cost is too great for my well-being. But then, you see what happened.' She indicated the birds in the tree with a sweep of her fingers. 'The lid accidentally came off and out they all hopped. My brother was even bitten by one, but I doubt he will sue you over it. Because, as I said, he is the best of men.'

Out of the corner of his eye, Thomas saw Evie cover her mouth. Oh, please do not let her laugh aloud.

'How did you know which of them had the sad expression, since they were never out front in the shop to be seen?'

'But I did see them, sir…with my third eye… I have "the sense", you understand, and I see things.'

Even for Minerva this was a bit much. All that was needed was to make an arrangement to pay for the shop-keeper's loss.

'Lord Rivenhall, you say.' The man stroked his chin, seeming to be deep in thought, no doubt counting the money he stood to gain from this misadventure. 'As much as I would like to give you that bird, miss, it has already been sold to another titled gentleman—all of the birds have.'

With that, Minerva burst into tears, ran to Thomas and buried her face in his chest.

'You see what the bird means to my sister. I will offer double what your customer offered—to make up for the inconvenience to you in having to cancel the first purchase.'

'Well, sir, I do not know if that is ethical. My client will be greatly disappointed.'

'Who is your customer? Perhaps I know him. I will be happy to speak to him myself,' he offered, well knowing there was no other customer.

'I'm sure there is no need to do that, sir. I believe though, that three times the cost will suffice.'

Minerva spun towards the man. 'You are no gentle-man, but a thief.'

'I do beg your pardon, miss, but those birds were in the crate last I saw them. Now they are in the tree. Who do you suppose is the thief?'

* * *

Of all the outrageous things to say!

Evie had been listening, biting back angry words and laughter. What an odd sensation to feel them both at once. Her emotions were all mixed up.

'You are the thief.' Evie allowed the anger to speak. 'Mr Pretender of Loving Wildlife While All Along Abusing Them! You are the one who hired someone to snatch them from their nests in the Amazon! Ripped the happy lives they ought to have lived away from them.'

'It's all right, Evie. I shall pay his extortion.'

She glanced up at Thomas, was stunned to see him grinning down at her.

'Do not, Thomas!' Evie strode up to the villain, stared him down. 'Not until we ask around and see who did purchase them and how much they paid.'

'I shall call the constable and let him determine who the thief is.' The man truly did have an ugly sneer. She believed it reflected his soul.

'I shall call him first!' How could she not counter his threat, even though it was the worst thing she could do since importing animals was not illegal but setting them free was? 'We shall let him determine who the victims here are.'

'The victims are my birds. Do you understand the great harm you have done them? They will not survive more than a week on their own.'

What? Was that true? It could be.

She glanced at Minerva, who looked as appalled as Evie felt. They ought to have planned the liberation more carefully. They had acted upon emotion, certain that freedom was the most important thing for a bird.

Minerva stared up at the tree, uncommonly silent.

'Come along, ladies.' Thomas laid one hand on her shoulder and one hand on his sister's shoulder and turned to lead them away.

He cast a glance back at the man. 'My solicitor will call upon you in the morning. I will pay a fair price for the birds and no more. And I will not sue you for the damage to my thumb.'

Was his thumb damaged? That would be the worst of this if it was. She took a quick glance at his hand resting on her shoulder. It was no longer red so she stopped worrying on that account.

But she was greatly worried about the beautiful creatures in the tree who would now need to fend for themselves. What had they done—given them their freedom only to have them perish as the price of it?

The kidnapper carried more guilt, but she was not innocent. She was left wondering—and a bit too late—what was worse, being doomed to a crate or doomed to the wilds of London?

She had felt a bond with those birds—they needed freedom as she had. She had set herself free, then had the good fortune to land in London, at Rivenhall. The parrots had also landed in London, but did not have Rivenhall to protect them.

Her heart cracked a little. She began to sniffle, tears of remorse streaking her cheeks. On the other side of Thomas, she heard Minerva sniffling.

'What are we to do now?' Evie asked, knowing there was really nothing they could do.

'Let me think on it overnight. I shall come up with

something.' Thomas's voice was deep, manly and commanding.

Oh, my stars. It hit her that there was nothing quite as attractive as a reliable man.

His expression grim, he lowered his brows, narrowed his eyes. He had to be angry at them for doing what they had done, for involving him in the mess. And yet, even scowling, she found him beyond appealing.

Had he taken this incident light-heartedly, made jest of it in the way her perfect man would have, her heart would not be fluttering.

Thomas Grant was not the type of man she'd always thought she wanted...but perhaps he was more. Caught up in everything, she had nearly forgotten the kiss.

Oh, yes, Thomas was more...much more.

Chapter Nine

The next afternoon, Evie carried Charm to the garden to play. Cuddling her to her heart, Evie decided she was the greatest hypocrite to draw breath. For all the care she gave Charm, she had released a flock of parrots to an uncertain fate. True, it was likely that, had she left them there, some would have died in the crate. But some of them would have found, if not freedom, at least safety in a home and people to care for them.

As soon as Minerva had suggested the rescue, Evie ought to have thought with her head and not her heart, should not have compared the birds' situation to her own.

She had felt just like them, doomed to a fate not of her choosing. Because she was not imprisoned in a cage, she had been able to make a choice for her future.

Had she been as helpless as those poor birds were, she would be bound and fettered right now to a husband she did not want, did not love or even choose.

From now on she was going to behave more reasonably. She was going to think things through and weigh the consequences.

But there was one thing…

Had she thought things through last night, she would not have kissed Thomas.

Why, she'd barely known who she was in that moment. Not in a million years would she have predicted she would do something so rash as to kiss a man who intended to court another lady. Furthermore, a man who was not at all the sort she had long imagined kissing.

'You can count on me not doing it again, Charm. You may dig your claws into me if you see me leaning that way.'

Oh…but it was a deliciously wonderful kiss, so unexpected and yet at the same time so anticipated. Now, wasn't that a silly thing to think? There was no way something could be unexpected and anticipated at the same time.

'But they might be,' she told Charm. Perhaps puzzling it out aloud would make sense of it. 'Because unexpected has to do with the brain while anticipated has to do with the heart. Anyone knows that the brain and the heart do not always agree.'

Perhaps it did make a bit of sense.

'I did not know I was anticipating it, but I must have been,' she admitted to the cat. 'Otherwise… Well, the important thing is that it was not a betrayal to Miss Brownton, since Thomas is not yet courting her.'

Not in the strictest sense, at least. It was his intention to do so, but so far they had only taken tea together. And that only once.

'Still, I will not kiss him again. It would not be pru-

dent.' She lifted Charm and peered into her eyes. 'And if
I attempt to rescue anything, you may hiss and scratch...
Although I did rescue you and that has worked well.'

Charm purred. She accepted the gesture as a thank
you.

She did not believe any of the birds were thanking
her. Even though the day was sunny, it was cool and a
slight breeze rippled through the garden.

What were they eating? Had they found water?

All her life, she'd felt herself to be a reasonably sensible person. For the first time, she suspected her judgement to be flawed.

After last night's mischief, she strongly suspected
that Thomas must think so too. No doubt the first
time she saw him she would lose her position. She had
thought so once before and had not, but this time it was
so much worse.

Because of her, Thomas stood to lose money. How
much would it take to appease the awful shop owner?
Just because a man was wealthy, as Thomas was, did
not mean he wished to part with his money. Especially
when the reason for it was not his fault.

Sharp pounding disrupted the peace of the garden,
drawing her from her thoughts. A hammer on wood,
she decided. It was coming from the direction of the
conservatory.

Curious, she walked that way.

The conservatory door was open. A man carrying
two hammers and a pouch of nails walked past the
opening, making his way around the corner.

Hearing voices within, she went into the conservatory.

'Thank you, Dr Randall. As soon as the first one arrives I shall summon you,' Thomas said to a tall, dig-nified-looking gentleman.

How peculiar.

Passing her on his way out, the fellow, Dr Randall, tipped his hat and nodded.

Was someone ill? She had not seen Minerva today.

'Evie!' Thomas spotted her and waved her over.

For the second time in her employment, she gathered herself to gracefully accept her termination. It was no one's fault but her own. At any point she could have advised Minerva that setting the birds free was not a wise idea.

But she had not and so must face the consequences.

'I'm sorry,' she said.

'I apologise,' Thomas said at the same time. And then, 'Well, we have been here before, haven't we? Each of us seeking the other's pardon at the same time.'

'I shall confess first,' she told him, feeling her in-sides flip. In worry, but also because she wondered how Thomas had grown more handsome just overnight. 'Once again, I beg your pardon for getting Minerva into trouble.'

'My sister says she got you into trouble. She talked you into it.'

'Even if she did, I consented. I felt quite righteous in letting the birds go, and now...' She was not going to weep. Except for that one little tear which escaped before she could call it back. 'And now the birds will perish.'

'You are not to blame, Evie. Neither is my sister. I was ankle-deep in parrots too.'

'You could hardly help it.'

'Of course I could. Had I insisted upon leaving the birds as they were, we would not be where we are now. The sad fact is, the shop owner will only purchase more birds. Our great act of liberation will do little good in the grand scheme of things.'

From outside the conservatory she heard more hammering.

'At any rate, I am doing what I can to ensure my birds do not perish. It is really all I can do.'

'Your birds? So you came to an agreement with that awful man. I hope you did not have to pay too dearly for them.'

'Not too dearly.'

'Oh, good then. I only wish… Well, it is not likely that the birds will survive.'

'It is highly likely that they will, now that they belong to me and not the shop owner. I am doing what I can to see to their safety.'

'But the birds are lost in the city by now.' She could not imagine what he could do about that.

'I have engaged wildlife experts who specialise in locating animals to capture them. The construction you hear is an enclosure, a proper environment for them to live in until I find good families who will adopt them. The veterinarian—you met him on the way out—will care for them as they arrive. As young as they are, he believes the birds will adapt to lives in captivity and, with the right families, be content.'

My stars, but this was good news. It was a happier outcome than she could have imagined. As long as the wildlife experts found them in time.

Perhaps she and Minerva ought to help in the search.

Helping would go a long way towards assuaging their guilt.

'Evie, you have no need to apologise to me for anything. Your heart was in the right place. You only meant to do good. But I must apologise to you.'

There was only one reason she could think of to make him feel the need to apologise.

The kiss. She desperately hoped he did not regret it.

Even though she did not intend to repeat the intimacy, to think he had not felt what she had in the moment would be crushing. She had been so certain that something magical had sparked between them.

Perhaps it had, but she understood that even if it were true it would not matter. Thomas did not require magic…would rather do without it.

At least it was what he believed. Quite wrongly believed.

Thomas was not a rake, but an honourable man. It was natural that he would feel guilty about kissing her when it was Lydia he ought to be kissing…in good time.

But there was a difference between feeling guilt and regret. In her mind it was true, at least.

Please, please, please do not let him say he regretted the moment she would cherish all her life.

'Will you show me the enclosure?' She stood up, hoping to divert him from dashing the memory of that lovely moment.

'Very well.' He rose, taking Charm from her. They walked in silence for a moment and then, 'Please forgive me for taking advantage of you last night.'

This was not a statement of regret, exactly. Maybe

he understood, as she did, that it had been a moment out of time and nothing more.

'You did not take advantage, Thomas. I imagine you know me well enough to understand I kissed you as much as you kissed me.'

Reaching the conservatory door, he stopped walking, staring down at her. His mouth opened and then closed…twice…but he seemed unable to summon words. It was several seconds before he began walking again.

'You are a lady, Evie,' he finally managed. 'You deserve more respect.'

Of all the nonsense. He made it sound as if she were a china doll on the shelf who might break with handling.

But he was who he was—and she liked who he was. Liked him more every day. And after last night? She would strive to store that kiss in its place as a sweet memory.

Walking around the corner of the building, she glanced sideways, trying not to stare at his handsome profile.

Hmm, well, she liked him even better than she had last night. The way he had taken charge of the parrot situation made her weak at the knees…so to speak.

He was a gentleman to the core, solid and responsible. How could she have ever dreamed such qualities would be so seductive? Not that she knew anything about seduction, but she was a woman and did have feminine awareness of such matters.

'You are a great gentleman, my friend, and so I understand your need to behave as one. And so I do accept your apology.'

On her part an apology was not required. However, she understood his need to offer it.

'Thank you, Evie. You may trust that I will not overstep again.'

'As long as you understand one thing. I do not regret our kiss. I intended to bring up the memory of it on cold, bitter nights when I have nothing else to occupy my mind.' She gave him a wink to make sure he knew this was meant in humour to lighten the moment.

He laughed. What a wonderful laugh he had. And the smile that went with it... My stars, but she was nearly undone.

Since he was set on courting someone else, she gathered her inner resources and tied them in a secure knot. She was absolutely not going to unravel. Even though she had led him to believe that what she said was in jest, she did intend to cherish the memory of the kiss and indulge in it from time to time.

It was going to take one happy-natured, ever-smiling fellow to make her forget kissing Thomas Grant.

'At least you need not fear such a dire fate, Thomas. I'm sure your nights will be wondrously joyful with Miss Lydia.'

Arriving at the spot where timber took the shape of a large shelter, he stopped walking, stopped smiling and stared down at her, seeming quite thoughtful.

'Mr Grant!' a voice called out. 'Mr Grant!'

Turning, she saw a man rushing around the corner of the conservatory dangling a bird cage in his hand. He lifted it high.

'I got two of the creatures, sir.'

Thomas took the cage from the wildlife fellow, thanked him and wished him success with the other ten.

'They will need to live in the conservatory until their shelter is completed,' Thomas said.

'I knew someone who had a parrot.' She walked with him into the half-framed shelter, thinking that two birds freely roaming the conservatory was not the best idea. 'It chewed everything. One morning they awoke to find the dining room table turned into kindling.'

'Heaven help me,' he muttered.

Heaven help her too. How was it possible for the man, over the course of a conversation, to become more handsome than even moments ago?

Perhaps because he had laughed.

Perhaps, as his friend, she ought to encourage that trait in him. He would be a happier person if he learned to laugh easily, like he had as a child. That was a cause she could devote herself to without causing anyone harm.

Except perhaps to herself. Years from now, when Thomas was merely someone from her past, she feared that the memory of his rare and joyful laugh would haunt her nights even more than his kiss would.

Thomas had used to be a sound sleeper. Recently he had become a restless one, a man who got out of bed to pace instead of being one who sank into his mattress then awoke with the sunrise.

This might be connected with the responsibility involved in running Rivenhall, if even for a short time. Standing in as Viscount was altogether different. For the first time, he truly appreciated what his father bore on a daily basis.

He had been vague, secretive even about his illness. Maybe because it was a minor ailment and nothing to be worried about. It might also be that there was a great deal to worry about and he did not wish to burden anyone with it.

Regardless, Thomas was doing what he could to reassure his father that all would be well. It was not easy. Especially when it came to his sister. He'd believed that engaging a companion would help. Now that he had, he was worried about what sort of trouble the pair of them would get into.

Worse…what trouble he would get into with them. He had not been himself last night. Breaking the law and feeling justified to be doing it. Not only had he done that, but he'd enjoyed it, laughed over it.

No wonder he was restless. Losing one's mind and the sober direction one had chosen for one's life would leave anyone sleepless.

Sober…thoughtful and honest—that was who he was. Once he turned his attention more fully to courting Lydia he would more easily stay the course.

Lydia would never leave him restless.

Indeed, it was not Lydia's face making him toss and turn on his bed. It was not the scent of her perfume making him stare at the ceiling. Rather, it was the memory of a whiff of lavender coming to him when he'd sat beside Evie at the circus.

No, Lydia would never leave him restless by her behaviour.

If, in the heat of the moment, he tried to kiss her,

what would happen? But, of course, with Lydia there would be no heat of the moment. He was fairly certain he would be no more tempted to steal an improper kiss than she would be tempted to kiss him.

But would Evie really bring their kiss to mind on cold, bitter nights when she had nothing else to occupy her mind?

No, the odds of Evie having nothing to occupy her mind—no one to occupy her arms—was remote.

She caused men to turn their heads wherever she went. She did not seem to notice it, but Thomas did. He could not quite work out why seeing those gazes upon her gave him such an itchy crawly feeling under his skin.

How he now longed for the days when his only concern was what William would do to embarrass the family.

The conservatory was partially visible from where he stood. Only the dome was in sight, moonlight shimmering on the glass roof. It would penetrate all the way down to the floor, giving the space an air of enchantment. His parents had used to enjoy spending time in there on moonlit nights.

Was Evie correct when she'd said that parrots could do damage? Dash it. He was not going to get any sleep until he could put the concern to rest.

He put on his robe and slippers, hurried downstairs then strode briskly along the path leading through the garden.

It was getting colder every night. He huddled into the robe, wondering what damage he would need to have repaired before his father came home.

When the Viscount returned, Thomas wanted him to find everything running as smoothly as when he'd left. If he could show him what a good Viscount he would make one day, it would set his father's heart at ease in the event that his health really was fading.

If his father came home to find everything running well, that he was courting Lydia and with Minerva taking an interest in marriage, it might go some way to ease whatever was wrong.

Perhaps he would host a soirée to move things along that way. Nothing grand, but an intimate event where his sister might become attached to a handsome young man. A poetry reading, perhaps, or a musical evening.

Arriving at the conservatory door, he held his breath. Please let there be no damage to the place his father had so lovingly built for his wife.

Slowly, fearfully, he opened the door.

'Come to me, you pretty baby,' he heard and then kissing noises. 'Oh…you poor sweet thing. Do you miss your mother? I miss mine too.'

He opened his mouth, closed it…sucked in a breath and then let it out in a silent whoosh.

He stood still, struck dumb in shadow.

Have mercy, but Evie was not struck by anything but moon glow coming through the glass roof. It illuminated her sweet, shapely figure within the fine-spun fabric of her nightgown. From where he stood there was a whisper of what lay beneath, but a whisper he heard rather loudly.

She was kneeling, her arm raised towards the bird, who peered down at her from the branch of a large bush.

He ought to retreat.

Ought to but could not.

Fascinated in what she was doing, as well as how she looked doing it, he wondered if the wild bird was really going to respond to the tender urging in her voice. No matter how inappropriate it was for him to be watching in secret, he had to know.

'Come now, sweetling, only a few more steps.'

The bird hesitated, but Thomas's foot jerked. He missed his mother too. If he came to her, would she comfort him in the same affectionate tone?

The bird ruffled its feathers then stepped onto Evie's arm. It imitated the kissing noises she had been making. She drew the bird closer so that it was inches from her face. All the while she cooed sweet words to it.

It was time and past to retreat. And yet—

'You are a very lucky chick,' she said softly to the bird. 'If it were not for Thomas Grant you would be in very dire straits. He is a wonderful man...kind and brave. I know you would like to be chewing the limb of the orange tree, but it is not how we shall repay him, is it?'

Him—kind and brave? He did not know anyone else who thought so. More likely he was known as being serious and unsmiling.

However, he was smiling now. In fact, he had smiled more in the short time that he had known Evie than he had in the past...well, he did not know how long, but ever since seeing her with pollen on the tip of her nose he had smiled more often.

The other bird, the one perched on the limb, side-stepped closer, cocking its head to peer down at Evie.

Did it recognise her as an angel? He did—in the

way she spoke and the way she acted. Not in the way she looked, though. Even with the halo he imagined shimmering around her curls, she did not resemble a saintly being.

Unbound for the night, her hair fell about her shoulders, tumbling in a red-blonde wave down her back. The sight was nearly ethereal—yes, nearly, because in that moment enchantment and earthiness balanced on the head of a pin.

He needed to get his feet to carry him out of the conservatory because, while the halo was imagined, the curves that moonlight hinted at were not.

No angel, Evie Clarke was every bit a woman…a quite desirable woman.

She set the bird down then turned her attention to the other young bird.

'Hello, sweet baby, would you like to sit on my arm like your…is it your friend or your nest mate, I wonder?' The bird did not move, but stared at her. 'If I need to spend the night here in order to keep you from chewing, it is what I shall do.'

She would? Why did the notion warm him?

'Thank you for that, Evie. I will stay with you,' he said, stepping out of the shadow, his foot all but poised over a hornet's nest.

'Thomas! Hello.' She reached for her robe, which was puddled on the floor next to her. 'What are you doing out here this time of night?'

'I remembered what you said about the birds chewing.'

'It is kind of you to offer, but you know as well as

I do that you cannot stay. Besides, I don't mind being out here.'

And he did not mind being out here either. Thomas would like to sit…well, not on her arm, but within the curve of it while she spoke tender words to him.

Funny that he had never realised how much he missed tender words. His mother was the only one who'd ever spoken to him with that particular warmth in her tone. It had been far too long since his heart had warmed to them… If he stayed perhaps…

But no… Even though he had offered to stay, he had spoken out of turn. It would be wildly inappropriate for him to do so. With his emotions vacillating, one moment seeing Evie as an angel and the next seeing her as a seductive woman…although innocently so…he should not be here.

But he was becoming rather accomplished at making mistakes these days. He must simply trust his sense of honour to see him through.

Simply? He could not imagine why that word had anything to do with how he was feeling. It made it seem that behaving in an honourable way was easy.

For the first time ever he did not trust his honour to prevail.

Evie was his sister's friend, a paid companion—a member of the household. She was forbidden to him even if he were not set on courting the woman next door.

'Thomas, there is no need for you to stay.'

And every reason for him to leave. Only…he did not wish to.

'There is every need. This is Rivenhall's conservatory and the birds up to mischief are my birds.'

'They would not be yours had I talked your sister out of setting them free.'

He felt a smile rising in him again. 'Ah, but I have not had such fun in longer than I can remember. It was worth every penny.'

Even in the dim light he could see her blush because there had been more than fun between them in those moments. There had been a kiss, which was worth far more than whatever he'd spent on the parrots.

Not that he could kiss her again. If he looked out of the glass dome of the roof he could see the peak of the roof next door. That was where his attention should be focused. Not on a past and brief delight, but on the future.

'You may return to the house. I will remain here to watch them.'

'I'm doing more than watching them. I'm winning their trust. If you wish to find them homes, they must learn to be comfortable with people.'

'I will do it.'

'I do not think—'

'That I can? Of course I can. Watch this.'

With a determined stride, he approached Evie, knelt down the way she was doing. Surely this could not be too difficult.

He held his hand out to a bird. 'Come here to me.'

The bird tried to nip his finger. Which he barely noticed. How could he when the scent of lavender tickled his nose…when it made his heart thump hard against his ribs?

'I do not think it appreciates being commanded, Thomas.'

'It was the same thing you said to it…or did you say it to the other one?'

'It hardly matters which one. They respond to the tone of what is said, not the words.'

He knew that to be true since he'd responded to her words, but a moment ago in the same way the birds had. If he did not leave the conservatory this instant he would begin making kissing noises…and not to the young parrots.

'I am perfectly fine out here, Thomas. The fire is lit and I have all the company I need.'

Good then…although he wished that she wanted him to be her company.

But really it was better she did not.

He stood. 'I wish you goodnight then.'

'Goodnight, my friend.' Her smile made the dimple in her chin dance. It made her round eyes sparkle, which made him…

Well, he did not dare even think what it was. Not if he wished to make it out of the door of the conservatory behaving as said friend would behave.

Giving one last nod, he stepped into the cold night and closed the conservatory door.

Closed the door on what his heart imagined doing. Which was forgetting propriety and indulging in the companion's company.

But that was simply not who he was. The future Viscount must be beyond reproach. Because of that, the future Viscount would live with memories, would behave as he was expected to.

He would not recall the memory of Evie consoling

the birds. He would dismiss his longing to hear such tenderness directed at him.

Perhaps, once he got to know Lydia better, he would find her to be as compassionate. There would be no need to bring up memories of Evie Clarke on cold, bitter nights.

Hunching inside his robe, he thought the night had grown decidedly more bitter than when he'd come outside.

Chapter Ten

Three days after the first parrots had arrived at Riven-hall, the enclosure was complete. For the most part the hunt to find the birds had been successful. Two of them were still unaccounted for, which did not rest easy on Evie's heart.

She sat at the breakfast table, her chin propped in her hand, weary to the bone. She had not slept for two nights, having spent them in the conservatory making sure the birds did not destroy Lord Rivenhall's special place. As she understood it, the indoor garden had been a very special gift for his wife.

Since no one else had come down for breakfast yet, she closed her eyes.

Oh, what bliss. To just sit and let her mind drift was a relief. Staying up all night then making social calls all day was enough to wear one down.

It should not come as a surprise to find that her mind drifted to Thomas. Unless she made a point of keeping it busy elsewhere, that was where her thoughts tended to go.

Just now they drifted to an image of his smile...how very pleasant it was...and what she could do to make him use it more often.

She could recite jokes if she were skilled at it. Or she could...um...what else...? Dance...sit on clouds... float—

Her head jerked. My stars! She had fallen asleep sitting upright at the table. There was a slice of ham on her breakfast plate. She cut a piece, chewed vigorously.

Thomas was hosting a gathering in two days. She needed to have enough energy to keep her eyes open throughout.

There was to be a poetry-reading by a local poet and music performed by a gifted neighbour. Other guests would be invited to sing as well. From what Minerva had told her, Lydia would be singing.

Evie hoped she had an enchanting voice because, for all that it was uncharitable to think so, a lovely voice might be the only thing exciting about the lady.

Yesterday, Thomas had invited her and Minerva to walk in the park with him and Lydia. Having watched the two of them together, she'd come to the conclusion that Thomas was going to be dissatisfied in his marriage.

Or, if not dissatisfied, at least not blissfully happy.

If one were to commit one's life to another person there needed to be some bliss involved, a dash of excitement at the very least.

Unbelievably, Thomas seemed to be content to have a wife who would occupy the perimeter of his life. There must be something she could do to save him from that fate...although she could not imagine what.

That sort of understanding must come from one's own heart or it was worthless. Besides, it was none of her business whom he chose to wed.

Mmm…it felt so wonderful to close her eyes again. Perhaps this afternoon she would nap in her chamber. Minerva was spending the day with friends and so she would be free to stretch across her bed and indulge in a doze for an hour or two.

She yawned. Odd images paraded across her mind which had nothing to do with anything logical. She must be falling asleep again.

'Evie,' she heard a voice whisper. It was Thomas's voice… How lovely this dream was becoming. She could nearly feel warm breath rush past her ear, tickle her hair.

'Evie!'

She jerked, her chin slipped off her palm.

'Were you asleep?'

'Oh, good morning, Thomas. I was simply resting my eyes.' She blinked, smiled. She would like to think he smiled back, but a twitch at one corner of his mouth hardly counted as that.

He set a plate of food on the table then sat across from her.

'Tonight you will not spend the night with the birds, but in your bed,' he stated, a vision of viscountly authority.

'Perhaps you are right. I imagine they can do without me for an evening. Now that their enclosure is finished the conservatory should be safe enough.'

He muttered something under his breath. She could

not tell exactly what it was but it sounded rather like 'so will I', which made no sense whatsoever.

As if suddenly realising he had muttered a secret thought aloud, he stared at her then blinked. A flush crept from his collar to his cheeks, settled into blotches on his cheeks. Something about his expression was oddly endearing.

The reason he was blushing might be that he was hiding something from her...not that she could think of what it could be.

But perhaps she could if she allowed herself to indulge in a fantasy about what might have happened had he remained with her in the conservatory that night.

Surely he was not imagining. It would not do for her to do so either.

To change the subject, she asked about his plans for the day.

'There is estate business to see to and later, in the afternoon, I am going to search for the last two parrots.'

'Have the wildlife men given up?'

'They are committed to another assignment for the next few days. But they have tracked the birds to a cemetery not far from here. The word is that a nasty storm is on the way. I feel bound to find the birds before then.' He picked up a piece of toast and buttered it while looking at her. 'What are you and my sister doing today?'

'She is busy with friends for the day.'

Oh, joy! She was suddenly wide awake. 'I will go to the cemetery with you!'

'I do not think—'

'I insist upon coming.' Brave words... However,

the decision was up to him. 'Please, Thomas—I have been wanting to help search—needing to, for the sake of easing my guilt over everything, but the time never presented itself. I promise I will not be any trouble at all.'

He shook his head, the message in his eyes a clear no.

'You will not know I am there. You will go one way and I will go another. I will be a great help.'

Something shifted in his expression. Something she felt rather than saw. That was interesting. She hardly knew what to think about it. She had heard of people reading one another's thoughts, but only after they had known one another for a long time.

No doubt she was mistaken in what she believed she saw since he had yet to respond. She prepared her mind to mount further argument.

'We shall leave as soon as my business is finished.'

Good then. She only wished she had been able to decipher how he felt about her coming along. His expression gave no clue one way or another.

Oh, well, if he was not happy to have her company at the beginning of the adventure, he would by the time they returned to Rivenhall. She intended to make a grand adventure of the outing.

Beneath Thomas Grant's staid demeanour, there was the little boy he had once been. That part of him needed to be set free. As it was now, he had blinded himself to carefree joy. If he did not learn to let the boy out to play once in a while, he would know no better than to propose to Lydia.

Evie and Minerva had both agreed it would be a terrible mistake.

* * *

It was nearly dusk when the driver delivered them to the gates of the cemetery. The Rivenhall business had taken longer today than Thomas had expected.

To top off the stressful day, he must now capture the birds. Hopefully, it would be easier than reviewing accounts had been. If not, it would be fully dark and raining before they got back home. The birds must be located at once. The veterinarian had been emphatic that they must have shelter before the storm hit. The weather would be far colder than they were used to.

His companion in the hunt must think him dour company. The frustration of the day's obstacles lingered in his mood.

He glanced across the carriage at Evie. She returned his gaze with a smile. Evie never seemed dour. In fact, if she took umbrage at his attitude it did not show in the least.

The driver opened the carriage door. Thomas stepped out and then gave a hand to Evie to help her down.

She grinned, then let go of his hand. Turning in a circle, she seemed to be taking her time studying the cemetery. Hopefully she would spot the birds and they could be on their way.

'This place is… Well, I imagine it is lovely in the morning but twilight makes it delightfully eerie.'

Was there such a thing—delightfully eerie?

Evie pressed close to him, shivering as they walked through the gates. It was hard to know if it was a serious shiver or done in jest. As far as he was concerned there was nothing delightful in the spooky half-light among the tombs.

Somewhere beyond the bank of fog pressing along the ground, twisting through the treetops, the sun was going down. Normally, twilight was lovely but here in this moment the light looked odd. Not dark, not light, but milky…opalescent in a way that was not normal.

They walked slowly past a large marble tombstone in the shape of an angel gripping a sword in its hand.

Evie smiled and winked. 'I half expect the dearly departed Mr Henry Jones to leap out and brandish that weapon at us.' A whirl of mist slithered towards them in an unnerving way. He wondered if Evie was frightened at the prospect of encountering an armed wraith.

Spending time in a graveyard was not his preferred way to pass the late afternoon…or early evening as it was quickly becoming.

'I might not mind if he could tell us where our parrots are,' he admitted.

'I may have spotted one.'

Already? How could she? This was a bit of good luck.

'Where?'

'Ah, but there is a cost to gain my knowledge.' She winked. The dimple in her chin matched the mischief in her eyes.

'What cost?'

Her quiet laugh illuminated the gloom. Evie hurried to the statue and pantomimed plucking the marble sword from the angel. 'A daring duel to the finish.'

'You have me at a disadvantage since I have no weapon.'

'Come along. Surely there is someone who will lend you one.'

He followed her, so focused on the fascinating sway of her skirt moving through the mist that he didn't completely feel the growing chill. But still he did notice, just enough to think they should accomplish what they had come for and go home. It was hard to know when the storm might blow in.

'Look, Thomas!' The figure on this tomb was of a woman, not an angel. It was extending a shovel as if she were offering it to him. He could not fathom why the figure would be in that pose unless she was offering the visitor to dig his own grave. Grim...but funny. The departed must have had a sense of humour.

'She must have loved gardening. She is offering you her shovel.' Evie's idea of the dead woman's motive was far better than his own. Her high spirits began to lift his mood. She pretended to accept the shovel. 'Thank you, Mrs Peabody. I shall return it to you shortly.'

She pantomimed handing him the tool.

'Face your fate, sir. That is, if you hope to gain the information I hold.'

Striking a pose, she brandished her invisible weapon, sliced the air between them.

'Did you hear how sharp the blade is, cutting through the fog?' she asked.

For a moment all he could do was stare. Her stance was bold. Without a doubt, she was the most beautiful swordswoman he had ever seen. She wore her hair loose tonight. It tumbled down her back, lively and happy looking.

He had never considered anyone to have happy hair, but there it was right before his eyes. The shovel went limp in his fingers. He nearly dropped a garden tool that did not actually exist.

'Thomas.' Evie posed her hand as if she were jabbing the tip of her sword into the dirt. 'If you do not engage in the game I shall feel a perfect fool.'

To ignore the call to play was more than he could resist. And he was not a man to make a woman feel a fool. It had been a miserable day and yet he now found himself grinning. How did she manage to do that to him?

'But you have me at a disadvantage, lady warrior. You have a sword, I have but a puny shovel.'

'Had you been quicker you might have had the sword. And truly, Thomas, if you allow your opponent to pick your weapon I do not know what else you may expect.'

He laughed aloud. The rumble rolling though his chest felt wonderful.

Life, the responsibilities of his position, would take him where he must go. But for this moment in time he was going to play with Evie in an increasingly creepy cemetery.

'Perhaps you failed to notice the sharpened edges on this humble tool?' He arched a brow to emphasise the point. 'I believe it gives me two razor edges to your one.'

What they ought to be doing was searching for the birds. It was the reason for the outing.

'Skill will win out,' she informed him with a grin that gave her the first round of the battle before she swung her sword. She would not be aware of it, but her smile sliced his heart neatly down the middle. 'Prepare to face your doom…in a graveyard with fog to smother your slain body.'

He moved to counter her thrust. She dodged, spun to avoid a vicious slice.

She lunged towards him in the same instant he lunged towards her. They bumped into each other. He caught her around the waist to keep her from falling.

'I shall rise from the grave...from this very dust to haunt you, Lady Evie. It is you who will face your doom.'

'I shiver to think it! Unhand me if you dare and we shall fight another round.'

Unhand? All of a sudden he noticed the way his arm curled around her waist, how his hand crept up to press her so tight against his chest that he could feel the *trip, trip, trap* of her heartbeat. And she was shivering.

Silently she looked up at him, her eyes wide and the game seemingly forgotten. Mist touched her hair, causing droplets to cling to the riot of curls.

Using his free hand, he trailed his fingers over the top of her hair, felt misty droplets grow slick under his fingertips.

All at once her breath hitched, her expanding lungs pressed her even closer.

He would not kiss her...would not even think it. Even though her lips were parted so temptingly, even though her breath puffed warmly on his face, he would not even imagine kissing her.

Except that he was imagining it...the fantasy so vivid he swore he felt the pressure of her lips making his mouth tingle. Perhaps it was tingling...the rest of him was. One wayward spark would set him completely ablaze.

'I am ready to face my doom now, Thomas.'

Her whisper was the wayward spark.

He dipped his head, lips on fire. *Evie...* His mind whispered her name.

'Evie... I...' He what? His head buzzed. His lips burned, her breath igniting the flame until...

Until he could do nothing but catch the fire and give it back to her in a kiss which caught him heart, soul and body.

She lifted on her toes, gave it all back to him.

An awful high-pitched squawk erupted overhead.

It might as well have been a ghostly shriek, so neatly did it jerk him back to his senses.

With a gasp, Evie pushed out of his embrace.

A cruel blast of cold rushed between them, robbing the space of the delicious heat that had swirled around and through them.

Glancing up, he saw the bird pacing back and forth on the limb overhead. It made enough of a squawking fuss to raise the dead...but no, perhaps not that.

'Quick, Thomas!'

Evie seemed to awake from the spell that had nearly undone them far more quickly than he did. Somehow that bothered him.

'Open the cage. When I have the bird, lift the box up to me.'

'Up?' he asked a bit stupidly, still feeling the effect of her lips beneath his.

She hiked her skirt over her knees, tucked it into the waist. 'Of course up. The bird will hardly come down to us.' She grasped a low-hanging limb, readying herself to climb.

He stopped her by laying his hand over hers. 'I will do the climbing.'

'It will not work if you do. I am too short to lift the box high enough.'

That was a point. He had to let her do the climbing.

The branch was not terribly high, but still he worried. It would be easy for her to slip and fall, given that everything was slick with mist.

Evie climbed, reaching the branch and bracing one leg on either side of it. She inched her way along until she was near the bird.

The wind came up, making the branch sway.

'Hello, you poor baby—come to me now.' It did not, but rather backed away from her.

'Do not go any further, Evie. The branch gets thinner and might not hold your weight.'

'It will. I have climbed over branches before so I know.'

'When did you climb over branches?'

She stared silently at him for a moment as if she did not wish to take the time to answer. Then she shrugged. 'When I was a child. My friend and I climbed trees every day. Now, get ready to take this poor cold bird.'

'I do not believe it will come to you. We ought to make another plan.'

'I cannot imagine what that plan will be. But it will come to me.'

He truly doubted that, since every time she spoke to the bird it waddled farther along the thinning branch.

But then she changed from speaking words to uttering some odd cooing, clicking noise.

To his utter astonishment, the bird sidestepped towards her. When she reached her arm towards it, it climbed on and made the same noise back at her.

'Thomas, please lift the cage now.' She did not change her tone, but spoke to him in the same soothing cadence, adding in a click or two so the young parrot would be soothed, he suspected. The lilting sound certainly soothed him.

She lowered the bird, continuing to speak to it. He lifted his hand and the parrot stepped trustingly onto his arm. Amazingly, it did not attempt to fly away when he placed it in the cage.

Either it trusted Evie or it was frightened of the coming storm more than it was frightened of him. The wind was rising now, rattling branches and howling around tombstones. For whatever reason it got into the cage, he was grateful because, logically, the poor thing had good reason to fear cages.

With the bird in the cage, he smiled up at Evie. 'Well done.'

'There is still another,' she said, then reached down for him.

Apparently, he was to catch her. He was to put his hands on her again. In such a situation he could not know for certain where his hands would end up... After that kiss a moment ago he could not know what his reaction would be if his hands slid to a spot they might inadvertently slide.

He had never fully appreciated the risks of gravity when it came to situations such as this. But why would he, since he had never been in a situation such as this?

'Thomas, this branch will not hold much longer.' Her urgent whisper snapped him out of considerations of what was proper. It would be beyond improper to let her tumble to the ground.

He lifted his arms to receive her. She grasped his forearms. Sliding down, she managed to gain her footing without grazing his chest.

He could only admit to being equal parts disappointed and relieved. Well, as an honest man he had to admit that it was not equal parts, it was weighted towards disappointment.

'Quick, let's get the other bird. It will be raining soon.'

She spun about, walking quickly in the direction they had come…to where the shelter of the carriage waited.

He picked up the cage and hurried after her.

'You know where it is?'

She glanced over her shoulder with a pretty grin. 'Of course. I told you I did.'

He had thought it all a game, but evidently part of it had been true.

If only he could be more like Evie, with the gift of turning a chore into a joy. He used to have it when he was a child. He remembered being able to turn any ordinary event into an opportunity for mischief. He and his brother had found fun in everything. He remembered feeling so happy then.

He no longer had that feeling. At least he had not until a few moments ago when he was battling Evie with his fierce shovel.

'There it is!' She pointed to a branch where a green spot moved among the autumn-coloured leaves. 'It is not as high up as the other one was.'

'I can reach it.' He would not risk her falling. Nor

would he risk himself falling. Not out of a tree—he did not mean that.

But what did he mean by thinking such a thought? Surely he did not mean falling in love. He liked Evie quite well, but love? He could not. He would court Lydia and please his ailing father.

'Teach me what to say to it.' He really had no idea why he could say what she did and not have the success she had.

He stood close to her, looking at her mouth. Once again heat sizzled through him. A splat of rain hit his face, followed quickly by another. It was all his imagination that the drops steamed on his skin.

'It is not the words so much as how you say them.'

He walked close to her, handing her the cage.

More rain splattered his face, wind whipped his hair.

'The other bird responded to those kissing sounds and clicks you made. Teach me those.'

'Watch my mouth, there is method to it.'

If only there was another way. Studying her lips, the way they rounded and puckered, damp with raindrops, was not the wisest course. But if he wished them to return to the shelter of the carriage before the storm hit in full he would need to learn to lure the bird.

Which would mean looking at her mouth.

Which would mean closing his mind to what he was seeing…feeling.

Evie pressed into the seat of the Rivenhall carriage, sighing inside her soul. It was now dark and she could not see Thomas all that well, but she could feel him.

Oh, my stars, she could feel him…the lingering press

of his kiss. That kiss had been…so…just…what was it? Forbidden, for one thing. Everything she had ever dreamed a kiss could be, for another.

Unlike the first time, she had not been innocent of what would come of kissing him. She had known. She had anticipated how he would make her feel, how every nerve would tingle in expectation of his deepening kiss…of the pressure of his fingers drawing her ever closer and all the while her heart swelling to a giant, yearning ache.

With rain pelting the roof and icy wind rocking the carriage every which way, she ought to be cold. Instead, she felt rather that her clothing was sweaty, cloying, that she needed to loosen her collar to keep from suffocating.

Thomas apparently recognised the cold temperature because he removed his coat and placed it over the birdcage to warm them.

To distract herself from the desire to slide across the carriage and snuggle under Thomas's arm, she peeped under the coat at the birds. They seemed well enough, despite all they had been through.

Convincing the second bird to trust Thomas enough to perch on his arm so it could be put in the cage had not been easy. What torture it had been watching Thomas study her mouth while she taught him to speak in kissing, cooing noises.

The wonder of it was that she'd refrained from throwing herself into his arms and demanding another kiss. He could hardly stare at her the way he had been and expect her not to act rashly.

He had only been staring in the name of capturing

the bird, she reminded herself. As far as she could tell, he was not suffering the lovely torment that she was.

In the end, her instructions had been for naught. Stare as he might, Thomas had not managed to copy the sound which would lure the bird.

Oh, no, it had taken Evie, standing cheek to cheek with Thomas...which was awkward, given that he was taller than she was...and then both of them making odd sounds to convince the bird to come down into the cage.

She could not imagine why the small creature had done it. They must have looked absurd.

Had the bird taken a second longer to decide, she was not certain how she might have reacted. How much longer she could have felt the scrape of his cheek on hers without embarrassing herself. Even now she was not certain the echo of that moment would not send her to the other side of the coach.

This outing had not unfolded quite as she had expected it to. Yes, they had captured the birds, and yes, they had fun doing it. She believed she had persuaded Thomas to relax and feel like a happy child again.

And what fun it had been!

An imaginary duel in a spooky cemetery... Well, she had not had such a grand time in...perhaps for ever. Gazing across the carriage at Thomas, she wondered if the same was true for him. Lashing at one another with sharp invisible swords and wicked garden tools had been so much fun.

But then, laughing, they had lunged at one another, somehow ended up in one another's arms. And he'd kissed her. Childlike pleasure had vanished in a heated heartbeat. Everything had changed then. In the blink of an eye her heart had tumbled.

How long, she wondered, would the echo of that kiss linger?

There was but one thing she knew to do in order to ground herself again. She must open the door of cold reality and let it blow the dreaminess out.

'I wonder what Miss Lydia will sing at the soiree.'

It was hard to see Thomas's expression, but he did cock his head as if he were peering at her in confusion.

'Come again?'

My word, but the cab really was quite chilly.

'Minerva told me she will be singing for our entertainment. I assume she must have a lovely voice. I only wonder what song she will lend her skill to.'

'I cannot imagine.'

'Oh...then I wonder what she shall wear. Some beautiful gown, I am certain. What is her favourite colour?'

'I'm sure I do not know that either.' Thomas leaned forward in the cab, his hands braced on his knees. This position made it easy to see his expression. Not that she could determine what was behind it. 'Evie, are you trying to avoid what happened between us earlier?'

'Here are the birds. We can hardly avoid our success.'

'You know very well that is not what I mean. You are avoiding the fact that we kissed again. But it happened and the reason for it must be faced.'

Perhaps, but there was every chance that his reason and hers would be entirely different, which would mean discussion would leave them more confused than ever.

At least it would leave her confused. She could not

admit how attracted to Thomas she was since he was not the sort of man she was attracted to.

Since she could not explain this to herself, she could not discuss it with him.

'Why do you think it happened, Thomas?'

'It is rather simple really.'

Was it? For him perhaps, but not for her.

'I have not had a great deal of unrestrained fun in my adult life, Evie. You gave that to me.'

'You kissed me out of gratitude, then?' It had been rather scorching gratitude, in her estimation.

'No...it wasn't that.' He clenched his fists, screwed up his face as if he were thinking hard. 'It is hard to explain it.'

She could explain it if she wished to, but she did not wish to. They were attracted to each other when they should not be. In a weak moment they had been undone by it.

'It was simply a reaction to the mood of the evening...to the thrill of our competition. We shared the bond of a common goal—the thrill of the hunt. We were overcome by the moment...and you are very pretty, my friend.'

She wondered if he missed the truth of what had happened because he chose to or because he did not feel the draw between them.

Since his life's path was not leading to her, it was for the best.

And so... 'You are quite handsome, my friend.'

He settled back into his seat. She gazed out of the window at streets illuminated by lamplight, glittering in the rain.

'And neither of us are as fetching as these handsome birds,' she said, hoping casual conversation would firm the ground she stood on...or the bench she sat on, as it were. 'Don't you wish you had bright green feathers and flashing eyes?'

'Indeed. I would impress my guests two days from now if I wore them. I could impress them with my squawk... Now, that would be fine.'

She could scarcely believe what she was hearing. Thomas Grant speaking in jest...making a joke.

Although he was not hers to be proud of, she did feel a sense of victory. She had set out to teach him how to have fun. Apparently, in a small way she had succeeded.

But was this turn in his sense of humour enough to make him realise that he needed more fun in his life than Miss Lydia Brownton was capable of offering?

That remained to be seen. Evie wondered if it crossed his mind that if he did attend the soiree in feathers and squawking, Lydia would want nothing to do with him.

Chapter Eleven

Thomas found himself grinning while his valet helped him on with his evening coat.

'Are you quite well, sir?'

'Yes, I am well. It is only…'

Feathers, bright green ones. It was all he could see when he gazed at his reflection in the long mirror.

Green feathers and his friend's sweet smiling face. No doubt Evie would be imagining him wearing them when she saw him enter the large drawing room to greet his guests.

This was something they had laughed over a few times since their graveyard adventure.

'I am anticipating an entertaining evening.'

He doubted the answer settled the valet's curiosity since he had never grinned in anticipation of an evening's entertainment before.

'Very well, sir. You are now presentable. I give you leave to enjoy your evening.'

With a nod of thanks, he left his chamber and went downstairs.

He actually did have great hopes for this evening. If even one of those hopes came to fruition he would consider the evening a success.

The birds were now up for adoption and he hoped they would find homes with his guests.

More important than that, he would introduce Evie to the young fellows with an eye to Minerva taking an interest in one of them. Naturally, it would be good for Evie to find a young man as well. She could not remain his sister's companion once Minerva wed. He wished very much to see Evie safely settled.

On the same note, he wished to see himself settled. The last of his goals for the evening was to promote his courtship of Miss Lydia Brownton.

He paused for a moment before entering the drawing room because a thought struck him...or a voice in his head, more to the point. It was Evie's voice, questioning him about why he had made his courtship of Lydia last on the list of importance in his mind when it ought to have been first.

He did not know why the thought came to him in Evie's voice, except that was the sort of thing a friend would say.

There was no time to dwell on that now. He had guests to greet...a lady to court. He settled his expression in a welcoming smile. He would approach Lydia first. That ought to send a message.

Entering the large drawing room, several gazes shifted his way. Guests smiled in greeting.

When his eyes sought Lydia, they settled on Evie. She acknowledged him with a grin. His smile transformed from pasted-on formal to warm and genuine.

Evie stood near the piano, along with Minerva and Lydia.

His intention had been to catch Lydia's eye first. He would need to work harder to give her his sole attention.

That would be difficult because Evie looked at him with humour in her eyes, with warmth and the knowledge of a shared secret. While everyone would be seeing him wearing a formal black suit, elegant and proper in every way, Evie, he knew, would see him wearing feathered eveningwear.

It felt good to share the unspoken joke.

What he ought to do was tell Lydia how the joke came to be. Would she share a chuckle with him?

Probably not. But he should find something humorous that they might share. That they might smile in secret over.

Crossing the room, he watched the three ladies smiling and chatting. There could not be three women more different from one another.

One sparkled in yellow, a ray of sunshine bringing more light to the gathering than the fire in the large hearth. Evie always looked cheerful.

One dressed in orange. As usual, Minerva gave the appearance of someone seeking adventure. He wished she looked as if she were seeking a husband.

The third lady was dressed in stately beige. As she always did, Lydia looked appropriate.

He ought to be gratified to see that. Lydia was everything Rivenhall needed and thereby everything he wished for.

And yet why was his gaze focused on Evie when it should not be?

Lydia was the lady his father thought highly of. Everyone did. He had never heard anyone point to one single thing about her that hinted at scandal.

Indeed, after all the family had endured due to William's past antics, Lydia was exactly the future Viscountess the Grant family needed.

It did not matter to him that she did not sparkle. It was better if she did not. No one would ever raise a brow at the family on her account.

Then his gaze shifted back to Evie. He reminded himself that being exciting did not matter...or it had not until the sunshine had swept into his parlour seeking employment, with a dot of bright pollen on her nose.

She was a good friend. One who did not hold his missteps against him. She had every right to. Kissing her had been so very wrong...on both occasions. He would be diligent not to do so again.

But wait... Something felt wrong about that. He should not need to feel diligent about behaving as a gentleman towards his friend.

He ought to give that more thought, only later.

Now he needed to see to the matter at hand. His father's health could only be improved if, when he returned, he found Thomas acting as a proper heir should, courting the proper lady his father preferred.

'I hope you are having a pleasant evening, Miss Brownton. I am delighted you could attend, even though this get-together was planned at short notice.'

'It is always a pleasure to attend a gathering at Rivenhall. You have such a beautiful home, Mr Grant.'

Good. It was important for her to think so.

'Would you care to accompany me to the refreshment room? Cook has outdone herself tonight.'

'How delightful. I would enjoy that.'

'Come along, Evie,' Minerva declared with a great smile. 'We shall go with them. Are you as hungry as I am? You do not mind if we come along, do you, Lydia?'

'Certainly not. I would enjoy your continued company,' Lydia answered.

Thomas watched her polite smile. It was very nearly pretty. Well, dash it! It was pretty, only in a demure Lydia way. All smiles were different. One was not preferable to the other.

'Thomas,' Minerva said, 'you must be famished as well. Lydia, you would not believe how much time we have invested in getting the birds ready for adoption... Well, mostly it was Evie and Thomas doing it. Hours upon hours of time.'

What did Lydia think of him spending so much time with Evie? Not that there had been anything inappropriate...at least, not lately.

If what Minerva had revealed about him and Evie spending time together bothered Lydia, she did not show it. Of course, she was a lady born and bred. She would not display negative emotions.

'I imagine it will be a great relief to you when they are gone.' Lydia turned her gaze towards Thomas. 'Did you know we can hear them making noise all the way next door? It must be troubling for you, being so much closer.'

For half a second what she said took him aback. The birds were loud, but he could not say it bothered anyone at Rivenhall.

As it turned out, he was not the one to escort Lydia into the refreshment room. Somehow their positions shifted so that his sister and Lydia went ahead, engaged in a lively chat about hats or some such thing.

He and Evie followed behind. Which was frustrating, since he needed to spend time with the lady he intended to court.

'I confess to being nervous, Thomas.'

'Why would you be? You look lovely this evening. Surely you have noticed the young men's attention on you and Minerva... I hope on Minerva.'

'Young men are always drawn to your sister. You can all but hear them sighing when she walks past, for all the good it will do them. Truly, Thomas, you cannot force her to pick a man. She will do so when she is ready and not before. I know you would like to be in control, but you simply cannot.'

He did not like to admit she was correct. Still, he held onto the hope that his sister would take to a young man soon.

'But why are you nervous, Evie?'

'For the parrots, naturally. Aren't you nervous for them? I wish so desperately for them to find families.'

'I do. As strange as it seems, we have become something akin to foster parents to them.' She really was beautiful tonight. She always was, but this evening she was even lovelier. Only a fool would fail to notice. Apparently not a single one of the young men in attendance were fools. 'We have done what we can. If some do not go to new homes they will be ours.'

For as long as she lived at Rivenhall, that was.

If he wed Lydia, would Evie remain his sister's companion? Live under his roof?

It was hard to imagine. And yet he would miss seeing her every day. He would miss Charm as well. Until Evie came he had no idea how much he'd enjoy having a playful cat in the house. Until Evie there were many things he did not realise he enjoyed. But that was not right. It was more that he had forgotten he enjoyed them.

Officially, Evie was his sister's companion, but she was his friend as well. For a man like him…friends were not so easily come by. People did not gravitate to him like they did to William.

But Evie had gravitated to him. Even though what she wished for in marriage…love…was not what he required, there was a bond between them. They were dear friends.

It might be an unusual relationship between a man and a woman, especially with the difference in their status, but she warmed his heart like no one ever had.

Did it mean he loved her? Of course he did. One did love one's friends, after all.

One did not kiss them, though. He was guilty of that two times over.

Had it only been one time, it could be excused as a momentary lapse of judgement… The second time, though? He might be more like William than he knew.

No…he would never give away kisses the way his brother had used to.

What then? Why had he kissed Evie twice? He had told her it was the result of the fun they had been having, had told himself that too.

Even if that were not true, he could never consider wedding Evie. He could not be the husband she needed…probably.

Lydia, on the other hand? Being a proper husband to her would be easy. They would have common expectations of their union. There could not be a more proper society match.

Besides, once he got to know Lydia better he was sure he would discover that she also enjoyed having fun.

The evening was ideal, if brisk, for a visit to the aviary. At least it would be ideal if she could ever get over feeling uneasy in company. She supposed one day enough time would have passed that she would no longer glance worriedly at everyone who visited Rivenhall. It was far from likely that a familiar face from home would show up—expose her for the fraud she was. Giving herself a good mental shake, she turned her attention to having a pleasant evening.

Not everyone was eager to go outside, but enough of them were to make Evie hopeful that some of the birds would be adopted.

'It looks as if Lord Finley will take one,' she murmured to Thomas. She might be standing too close to him since she could smell… Well, never mind that. She ought to take a respectable step away, just in case anyone took notice of how their elbows were nearly touching.

Lord Finley lifted the bird perched on his forearm. Parrot and human gazed intently at one another, seeming to take one another's measure.

'Our Tillie will go to a good home,' Thomas assured

her. 'Lord Finley is a widower so the bird will get a great deal of attention.'

Our Tillie? Thomas looked at her with an expression which made her take that step. What was really behind that intimate smile? Probably not what she read into it.

'Mrs Muldrew is looking fondly at Petie-boy,' she noted.

With a discreet, exceptionally brief glance, she admired how handsome Thomas looked tonight. No doubt Lydia would swoon once Thomas began to give her serious attention. Once she understood he meant to court her she would probably become weak at the knees. Evie locked her own knees, since it was not for her to go all weak in the joints.

Even though his lady of choice had not come outside, she made her glance at Thomas appear casual. It would not do for anyone to guess what was in her heart and carry the observation back inside.

In her seemingly objective glance she saw a man who was greatly different than the one she'd met that first day. In the beginning, getting Thomas to smile had been difficult…rather as if it would hurt his face to do so. But now, on the rare occasion, he laughed aloud.

There was a glow in her heart for him, but also for herself for helping to bring about this change. However, it was not so much a change as an excavation. She had been diligently digging into his heart to bring that side of his character back from his childhood, where he had abandoned it.

If he noticed her smile at that moment he would assume she was pleased with what they were accomplishing with the adoptions.

Just as well. It would not do for him to guess how deeply she was becoming attached to him…to their friendship, she reminded herself.

A good friend was beyond price.

After a short time everyone returned to the house.

'Shall we go back inside too?' Thomas took her elbow. 'It is growing cold.'

'Thomas!' Mrs Muldrew hurried back down the path from the house. 'I hope you do not mind, but my house guest has only just arrived from the country. I left word for him to come over at once. He is a bird-lover and would adore seeing yours.'

A second later the guest stepped out from behind her, hand extended in greeting.

'But we have met before on a few occasions! Lord Haverly, it is good to see you again.' Thomas shook his hand.

Evie took a long step backwards, grateful for the shadow covering her face.

No! No! No! This was beyond disaster!

'Lord Haverly, you will remember Evie Clarke.' Thomas motioned for her to step out from the shadow where she cowered. 'You were quite correct in your glowing recommendation as companion.'

She stepped into the torchlight because there was nothing else to be done but swallow her heart and face her shame.

'Violet?' Mary's father stared at her, blinking, frowning. 'Can it really be you?'

Violet?

Thomas cast a glance about. He did not recall inviting anyone by that name, not that there was anyone to see but the four of them.

'Good evening, Lord Haverly.' Why was Evie's voice trembling? Why was she responding to the name Violet?

A dozen whys pressed upon him at once.

He squinted his eyes at her. She looked pale, her cheeks as blanched as bare bone.

Evie never looked pale. But…why had Haverly called her Violet?

'My dear!' Haverly rushed forward to embrace her. 'Your cousin is frantic with worry. Mary told him you had gone to visit friends in the city…but I am confused.'

So was Thomas. What in the blazes was going on here? Did Minerva know?

Haverly shifted his gaze to Thomas. 'What do you mean by my recommendation?'

'For…' He looked hard at who he had thought to be Evie. His heart felt cleaved down the centre. 'For this young lady to serve as companion to my sister.'

'I sign many things in the course of a day but…well, perhaps Mary…'

He shook his head, looking as perplexed as Thomas felt.

'I am afraid I do not understand, Violet. Why are you…and why would Mary…?' His voice trailed off.

Violet? If this was not Evie… He was caught in a whirling state of emotion—betrayed, angry, confused and bereft. All of those and all at once.

'But my dear—' Haverly dropped his hands from her shoulders '—what became of the friends you went to visit in Liverpool?'

Thomas had always assumed she'd come straight from Haverly's employ to his.

Evie, or whoever she was, pressed her lips together. Clearly, the woman was scrambling to make up a story. He knew her well enough to sense it. But then, he really did not know her at all.

'My friend is a miserable communicator. She neglected to inform me that they left for the Continent a week before I arrived.'

'But why did you not return home immediately? I do not understand. Why take a position as a companion?'

This made no sense. She'd gone to Liverpool to visit friends…with a letter of recommendation for employment? A letter of reference which Lord Haverly had no recollection of writing.

There was a moment of silence in which Evie chewed her bottom lip. Being caught out in lies, it was no wonder she found it hard to speak. She was a clever lady, but not clever enough to cover her deception.

Rather than admit to it, she spun about and took a dozen steps along the path. Coming to a sudden halt, she turned to look at the Viscount.

Her gaze passed over Thomas without pause. He had the devastating feeling that he had become invisible to her. Yet she had tears gathering in her eyes.

Remorse for her heartless deceit, no doubt. Thinking how Minerva was going to be crushed brought anger to the forefront of his emotional jumble.

'Give Mary my regards, sir.' She dashed at her cheek. 'And tell her I miss her.'

Mrs Muldrew cast Evie's retreating figure a quizzical glance. Somehow, in spite of what had just occurred, he could only think of her as Evie.

Who in the blazes was Violet?

'My goodness, but that was odd. I do not understand it at all.'

'Nor do I,' the Viscount answered. 'I am only happy to discover that nothing untoward has happened to her.'

Of all of them, Thomas was the most confused. Not just that, he was devastated in a way he could not have expected to be. He did not know who Evie was...except that she was not Evie.

'Come, Thomas.' Mrs Muldrew took his elbow. At the same time she took Haverly's elbow. 'You must show my dear friend your parrots. I'm sure he will want one.'

Towed along by Mrs Muldrew, he went towards the aviary, although he had lost heart in anything to do with the birds.

There really was nothing else he could do except terminate Minerva's companion's employment.

Perhaps she did have a reason for what she had done, but dishonesty was not to be tolerated. He would speak to his sister in the morning.

Tonight he would put Violet... Evie...from his mind and redouble his attention on a proper lady who would never stoop to deceit for any reason. Lydia, he would wager, had never told a falsehood in her life. She was a lady to the bone.

That was his impression of her, at any rate. He had thought the same of Minerva's companion at one time... only moments ago, to be precise.

Chapter Twelve

Evie did not return to the drawing room, but fled upstairs to the privacy of her chamber. It would be a bit much to hope that the people downstairs were not already speculating about her. It would be a wonder indeed if Lord Haverly was not discussing her mysterious appearance in London.

He must have been puzzled to find her here. Mary would not have told anyone where she was, especially her father. Lord Haverly, unlike her own father, clung to the outdated view that a lady ought to wed for society's good. She and Mary had overheard discussions between their fathers regarding marriage on more than a few occasions.

If Lord Haverly believed that Cousin Hubert was distraught with worry, he would return home and reassure the awful man that she was safe and where she could be found.

The emotion she'd held in check was finally released. She let out a great sob, fell face first on the bed and wept into the quilt.

She loved her life here. She loved this beautiful mansion which had felt like home from the first time she'd climbed the front steps.

More than that, she loved Minerva, who had become as dear a friend to her as Mary was.

She loved Thomas, who was as dear a friend as…as no one had ever been. Her feelings for him were complicated. She did not understand them. There were moments when she wanted to throw herself into his arms… kiss him until he forgot he meant to wed for his father's approval…which was an outrageous reason.

She had hoped to show him that…but now?

No…it was unlikely that he considered her a friend any longer. Friendship required honesty. Thomas Grant was a man who valued honesty and social propriety above all else. Even above his own happiness. There was little hope, rather none at all, that he would overlook her lies.

By morning she was sure to lose Minerva's friendship as well as gainful employment.

Something sniffed her hair, purred in her ear.

Charm—she still had a friend. The kitten loved her no matter what. Sitting up, she wiped her eyes, hugged the kitten close.

'I cannot imagine what we will do. You must be prepared because we are sure to be sent packing tomorrow.'

In the instant a new bout of sobs constricted her throat, her chamber door opened. Minerva slipped inside, clicked the door closed behind her then leaned against it.

'You are quite the topic of conversation down below.'

Did Minerva hate her like her brother must? If so she could not bear it.

'What are they saying?' She did not really want to know, it was only that she thought she ought to. Gossip could be cruel and she hated to see it land on Rivenhall yet again. And because of her!

'It is all very hush-hush, but everyone is wondering who Violet is.'

'I am so sorry, Minerva. I never intended to bring trouble to your family.'

'I would not call it trouble so much as interest.' Minerva came to the bed, then sat down beside her. She glanced for a second at the tear tracks on Evie's cheeks, but did not remark upon them. Lifting Charm out of Evie's arms, Minerva nuzzled the cat under her chin. 'And really, ever since William married things have been rather dull around here.'

'I believe that is how your brother prefers it.'

'He only thinks he prefers it. I have seen him change since you came. Sometimes he smiles when he looks at you.'

'That does not mean anything.'

'It means a great deal, but not as much as kissing you does. When you put the two together, I guarantee it means he is smitten.'

'If he was, he no longer is…and how did you know he kissed me?'

'I was there, standing in the alley waiting for you to finish. Believe me, my brother is careful with his kisses. Thomas is as smitten as they come.'

'It does not matter if he is. He is going to wed Lydia. And tomorrow he will terminate my service.'

'You are my friend and shall remain so, no matter if you are paid to be or not. But do not worry, you will not lose your position.'

'You know how your brother values truthfulness, and I lied to him.'

'He can be a bit of a stickler for the rules, but he is more used to fibs than you know.' Seeing Minerva's smile felt like a balm smoothed on her aching soul. 'William and I were... Well, you can guess, but the important thing is that he will not dismiss you because if he does I shall threaten to go with you. Father would be furious if that happened.'

'You are a loyal friend, Minerva. The dearest I ever had.'

'And you are mine...but I am on pins to discover who Violet is.'

'She is me—Violet Evie Dumel. Clarke was my mother's name before she married.'

'As scandalous lies go, that is not much of one.' She loved Minerva for appearing disappointed.

'But it was. My intention was to hide my identity.'

'I am sure you had a brilliant reason for it. I cannot wait to hear what it is...if you wish to tell me, naturally. I promise I am discreet.'

'If anyone will understand why I did it, you will.' She hoped and prayed she would, because she did not want to lose Minerva's friendship. Income be hanged. While she did need the money, some things were beyond price. 'I was running away from a marriage that my cousin Hubert was determined to foist upon me. You have met Lord Haverly?'

Minerva nodded. 'He seems confused about why you are here. By the way, he is taking two parrots home with him. One for him and one for his daughter.'

'Yes, well, Lord Haverly's daughter, Mary, is the one who helped me escape. We have been close since we were children. I do not know what I would have done without her. She is the one who wrote my letter of reference.'

'I think Mary and I would get along famously. But I imagine your father's cousin must be a beast.'

'Both he and his wife are. They are forcing a lecherous old man upon me. And why, you might ask.'

'Oh, Violet… Evie… I need not ask why since the answer is obvious. Money.' Minerva set Charm on the mattress, then stood up. 'They are the ones who forced you into this small deceit. They are at fault.'

'So I am innocent?'

'As a newborn babe. Now, I must go back downstairs. If the situation were different I would insist you come with me, but we do not want the Viscount thinking about you more than necessary. He must believe you are leaving Rivenhall. We do not want those wicked relatives of yours to come here seeking you. I shall spread word that you are going to…'

'I am going to Liverpool because my friends have returned.'

'That will do.'

'But, Minerva, I want you to know how desperately I will miss you.'

Minerva paused beside the door. 'No, you won't because you are not actually going anywhere.'

'It will not be safe for me to stay here.'

'You are safest here, where Thomas and I can watch over you.'

'Thomas will not want me here. Besides, he will be busy courting Lydia.'

'So he thinks.' With that Minerva laughed, stepped into the hall and closed the door behind her, then opened it again. 'I still do not know what to call you.'

'Evie.' She felt Evie to her soul.

'Do not worry, Evie. This will all come out right in the end.' With that, Minerva closed the door again.

Evie sighed. If only she had half of Minerva's confidence. But when all was said and done, it was Thomas who would decide whether she stayed or not.

She did not believe he would keep her on. He put such value on integrity, truthfulness and honour. No doubt he regretted that he'd ever met her.

Which was something she would never do—regret knowing him. Knowing Thomas only pointed to how correct she was to want to wed for love. If that meant she loved him or not, she could not be sure. It might and yet she would be better off not loving him in the way a woman longed for a man.

Especially since the man she longed for was downstairs, perhaps already on bended knee. Lydia's father was here tonight, so he might have asked for permission to wed her.

But no, her mind was wandering to the improbable. Thomas would not rush. He would do everything in its proper time.

Such as sending Evie away in the morning. He would

consider her departure from Rivenhall more than appropriate.

Perhaps it would be.

Entering the drawing room, Thomas's intention was to seek Lydia, to give her his full attention for once and not let his mind wander to Evie. He did not see her at first, but then the crowd in the drawing room shifted and he spotted her, sitting with Viscount Haverly and Mrs Muldrew.

He hated to think of what might have happened, where his heart might have wandered, had the Viscount not arrived. The state of his emotions had been all but tumbling off the pedestal of reason. Good sense, long-held values, had nearly crashed at the feet of the deceptive Miss Clarke. If that was even her last name. Since he did not wish to use the familiarity of calling her either Violet or Evie, Miss Clarke would have to do.

'Ah, Mr Grant.' The Viscount stood to greet him, then sat again when Thomas did. 'Once again I thank you for allowing me to take two of your birds. They are such fascinating creatures. I do enjoy them, even though I had one years ago that got loose and chewed up my dining room table in the night.'

Miss Clarke had told the truth about something at least. Not that one truth changed his opinion of her character. She might be as lovely as sunshine and fun to spend time with... Indeed, he had let down his guard and laughed with her. Which he now regretted because, for all that he had enjoyed it in the moment, he was suffering now.

In the morning she would be dismissed from Riven-hall and he would get on with his life as it had been.

'I do not see Miss Dumel.' The Viscount glanced about. 'I was hoping to have a word with her.'

Dumel, was it?

'I believe I saw her going upstairs,' Lydia said. 'Isn't it odd that she gave her name as Evie Clarke? Everyone is wondering why. But I imagine she had a reason for it.'

'But Evie Clarke is her name, in a sense.'

'What sense is that, sir?' He wondered if his tone sounded as snappish to others as it did to him. He did not wish to appear peevish and ill-mannered. Which was exactly how he felt.

'Violet Evie Dumel is her name—Clarke was her mother's maiden name.'

'They are all lovely names,' Mrs Muldrew put in. 'If they were mine I would use every one of them. I only have the one name, so not nearly as much fun.'

The fact that Evie was among her names did not mean she had not used it to deceive him. For all that he was troubled to discover Miss Dumel's duplicity, it troubled him even more to be troubled by it.

Confound it—did that even make a whit of sense?

Only if, in spite of things, he did care for her. Otherwise he would not be troubled.

'May I ask something of you, Mr Grant?'

'But of course.' He was glad to have the conversation turn another way. He would rather be thinking of Lydia and getting to know her better.

'When you discover where in Liverpool Miss Dumel is going, will you let me know? I'm certain her fiancé would like to know.'

If there was still a chair supporting him he would be stunned to know it.

Evie…engaged? He had kissed a woman who was promised to someone else!

This was what came of indulging in passion.

Knowing what he now did of Evie pointed out how correct he was to wed for duty.

It was early, the sun barely risen on this cold, drizzly morning.

Evie—she no longer felt like Violet and would not go by it any longer—stood at the head of the stairs with a valise in one hand and Charm on her shoulder.

'Here we go, Charm.' She stepped down one stair. 'We shall take a hansom back to the hotel then take a day to decide where we will go.'

She took another step, glancing below at the home she had come to love. The servants were already up and about, having lit the hearths and opened the curtains to the grey day.

Naturally, it would be grey to match her spirits.

'I am sorrier than you know to be taking you away. You will miss everyone as much as I will. But we shall settle somewhere else.'

The scents of breakfast being prepared wafted down the hallway. In spite of her mood, she was hungry. However, she could not go to the kitchen to beg a morsel or Cook would know she was leaving.

If anyone knew, they might alert Thomas. Although, chances were, he would prefer to have her slip away rather than having to bid an awkward farewell to a friend who was not a friend at all.

It was cowardly of her, to be sure, but she simply could not find the words to say goodbye to him. Not only because of her guilt but because it would be appropriate for her to offer him best wishes on his courtship of Lydia. Perhaps it would be.

Regardless, the words would stick in her mouth because, to her way of thinking, she would in truth be wishing him ill. Not because she wished that for him, but because she knew that he was going to end up miserable if he wed Lydia.

She had come to know the man he was at heart and she understood that in the end he would not be happy in a marriage which only fulfilled duty, no matter that he thought so. But it was no longer up to her to reveal to him the forgotten joy of who he used to be.

Perhaps, had she been honest from the first about who she was and why she needed a position, things would be different now. Or not. In all likelihood, she would have been turned away without an offer of employment. Knowing Thomas, he would not welcome potential scandal to Rivenhall's front door.

A front door she was now closing quietly behind her.

Evie decided that she would rather be a kitten than a human. It appeared that Charm was as happy to play in the small room of an inn as she was in the vast spaces of Rivenhall. She climbed the curtains in joy. Apparently the kitten was already over the heartache of having to leave such an inviting home.

Evie did not believe she would ever be over it.

'Violet Dumel,' she muttered, coming again to the

conclusion she was more Evie than Violet. 'Who am I, Charm?'

She had been comfortable all her life as Violet. Now she did not feel like the woman who had run away from home.

Falling in love would change a person.

She went to the window, plucked Charm off the curtain, then held her close to her heart while she gazed out.

'I will tell you something. I do love Thomas. It is time I faced the fact. Oh, I tried to pretend it was something else because it is not the thing to love a man who means to marry someone else.'

She must have squeezed the kitten too hard because it scrambled out of her arms then hopped to the floor.

'When I used to call him my friend I do not know who I wished to fool more, myself or Thomas. I suppose it does not matter what I admit to you, Charm, since I will never see him again.'

Charm sat on the middle of the rug, cleaning her outstretched leg with her raspy pink tongue.

'I can see you agree...or do not care. I love you, missy, but I need a human friend. I need Minerva. I need Mary.'

Since she was unlikely to see either Mary or Minerva again, she sat down on the bed, crossed her arms over her chest and felt sorry for herself. Truly, it would be better to be a kitten.

A sudden rap on the door startled her. She leapt to her feet.

No, no, no! It was impossible for Hubert to have found her so quickly. Unless Lord Haverly had sent a wire last night and her cousin had taken the first train to London.

Worse than seeing Hubert would be opening the door to Baron Falcon. But of course it could not be either of them. It was only her fear suggesting it.

But there was someone pounding insistently at her door. It must be one of the staff bringing more fuel for the fire. But they tended to tap discreetly, not pound as if they wished to knock the door down.

To avoid that from happening, she crossed the room and opened the door a crack. A large hand curled around the edge, forced it open all the way.

'Thomas!'

He pushed into her room. Charm dashed for him, climbing his trouser leg.

She backed up, her hand to her throat because…

'What are you doing here? How did you find me?'

'How is irrelevant. What I am doing here is not.'

His scowl was so intense she nearly regretted being in love with him. She preferred a cheerful man. She should have remembered it while she was losing her heart. All right, she had remembered. She had simply chosen to ignore it.

'Very well, Thomas, so what are you doing here?'

'I have come to hear the truth, if you are capable of telling it. I would have the reason you lied about who you are as well as the fact that you are engaged.'

'I am more capable of telling the truth than you are of hearing it. If I thought you would understand perhaps…but never mind. No matter what my cousin says, I do not consider myself engaged. The reason I did not give you my complete name is that I ran away to prevent being married. I shall make my own way in the world rather than submit to injustice.'

'Marriage…injustice?'

'Quite, but I suppose a man like you would see it differently.'

She might tell him the whole of the matter—that she was all but being sold to a lecherous old goat of a man—if not for the fact that he was scowling at her. Apparently he did not believe, as a woman, she had a choice.

A clock on the wall tick, tick, ticked while Thomas stared hard at her.

Hard rain slammed the window all at once. Startled, Charm arched her back at the glass and hissed.

'Gather your things. We are returning to Rivenhall.'

'You are returning to Rivenhall. I am not.'

He crossed his arms over his chest, his stance unyielding, as if she had not spoken—as if he were waiting for her to do his bidding.

'It is not proper for you to be in my room.'

'Nor is it proper to deceive one's friends.'

Briefly, some emotion darkened his eyes, darkened them more than they already were, that was.

She thought it was pain. Grief for wounding him nearly made her turn away. But no, it would be cowardly to avoid the consequences of her actions because, in truth, she had wounded him.

For all that she had hoped to avoid this moment by leaving Rivenhall early that morning, it was upon her.

While she was angry at him for not seeming to understand the reason she'd kept her secret, it did not change the fact that she was the one in the wrong.

Very well. 'I owe you an apology, Thomas. Would

you like to sit for a moment?' She indicated the desk chair on the far side of the room. She sat upon the bed because there was no place else.

Sitting on a bed in Thomas's presence was inappropriate, given the thoughts suddenly blossoming in her mind. She could not fathom why they should be. His expression certainly did not invite intimate thoughts.

She spread her skirt, smoothing the folds while she herded inappropriate images out of her brain.

Oh my... Another emotion crossed his eyes. She read it quite well since it was akin to what she had been thinking. These were emotions he should reserve for his future intended.

In the end, he did not sit, but indicated the valise on the floor with a tilt of his head.

'You may tell me more about the situation regarding your fiancé in the carriage if you wish.'

'As I said, he is not my fiancé.'

'No more lies, Miss Dumel. Or whatever name I should call you.' Thomas swept up Charm, tucking her into the large pocket of his coat. 'Let's go.'

'You cannot force me to go with you. You may call me Evie.' Not that he would need to since she was not going to see him after this.

Spotting her cloak on a hook, he snatched it then twirled it about her shoulders. He paused for a moment too long when he fastened it under her chin. Their gazes caught and held.

'If you wish to bring your valise, take it now.'

She refused to move. 'I do not know why you would wish to take me back to Rivenhall.'

'I do not wish it. It is for Minerva's sake.'

'I shall write to her once I am settled somewhere.'

'You shall settle at Rivenhall.' The man did have a determined glare, which he was accomplished at wielding.

'I shall not!' Her temper was beginning to rise. Just because she'd decided she was in love with him did not mean she was going to live in his house.

It was all the more reason not to.

'My sister is embroidering.'

'Flowers?'

'On handkerchiefs.' His severe expression softened somewhat. 'Please, Evie, she is not herself. I am worried.'

It was hearing him call her Evie which broke her resistance, not concern for his sister. She did not believe Minerva was languishing. Clever was what she was, clearly using Thomas's sense of brotherly loyalty to force him to bring Evie back.

But she would rather be there than anywhere else she could think of…and, truly, she did not know where she would go anyway.

She picked up her valise then followed Thomas into the corridor, along the hallway and down the dim stairwell.

'Wait a moment.' She stopped and pointed at the front desk. 'Thomas, I owe money for my stay.'

Thomas turned back and took her elbow. 'I took care of it. Let's go.'

'You should not have presumed to do that. I can take care of myself.'

His answer was to grunt—at her!

That high-handed attitude made her simmer under

the collar. At least she would count that for the reason she was simmering. But if she were to be completely honest—something she was not now known for—she would admit that the heat was coming from his hand pressing her elbow.

'You need not manhandle me, Thomas.' She forced her voice to sound outraged because she did not wish for him to know what was going on within her. If she did not want him to guess she was in love with him she would be forced to act yet another lie. 'I will come along since you give me no choice in it.'

'Thank you.' And that was the last he had to say to her on the long, tense ride back to Rivenhall.

Chapter Thirteen

Thomas felt he had been played for a fool. Not by Miss Clarke this time, but by his sister. He could not imagine why he was surprised by it.

Last night, coming up the path after fetching Miss Clarke, he'd spotted his sister in the window of the small parlour. Having cast her stitching aside, she was twirling about, a book in hand. His sister was the only person he had ever seen with the ability to read and dance at the same time. It was something she did when she was quite happy.

She must have heard him come in the front door because when he entered the parlour she was sitting on the couch, embroidery in hand. Given the tell-tale lump under the cushion, that was where she had stashed the book.

'Life is so dreary, Thomas.' She let out a dramatic sigh. 'I do not know what I shall do for the rest of my life with no companion to keep me entertained.'

'You sent me to bring Miss Clarke back to you. I have done it so you may stop moping.'

'That is grand.'

This was not the reception he had envisaged—the hero's welcome. Which he felt he deserved since getting Miss Clarke to return had not been easy. The carriage ride back to Rivenhall had been the worst journey of his life.

He was not used to Miss Clarke's silence, her sober expression. The one and only comment she'd made was that she did not appreciate being kidnapped.

Did the woman not know a rescue from an abduction? Had he not come to fetch her home—not home so much as back—who knew what might have become of her?

Now that she was safely under his roof, he could dismiss any further responsibility for her from his mind. She and Minerva could go merrily about their social lives and he would go about his. It was a large house and their paths need not cross all that often.

'Grand?' he pressed. He deserved at least a small amount of gratitude.

'Yes, wonderful.'

'Sometimes, Minerva, you try my patience. The weather is miserable, I have a dozen other things to do and I think you could at least express some gratitude that I brought your companion home without giving me a sarcastic comment.'

Minerva stood and walked up to him, giving him a hug. 'I am quite grateful. And you have restored her allowance?'

'I never took it away.'

'But it was assumed when you dismissed her.'

Heaven help him. 'You know very well that I did not dismiss her. She left when we were asleep.'

'That is neither here nor there, Thomas. But if you increase the allowance it will encourage her to stay.'

If money would smooth the situation over, very well.

'Done. But I will ask for a favour in return.'

She arched a brow at him in question.

'Please, Minerva, all I ask is that you put away that embroidery and never get it out again.'

'I shall try, but it will not be easy.' Then she laughed. 'You are the best brother alive.'

'Better than William?' He was teasing and she knew it.

'Different, but both loved. And do not fear, you will end up as happy as our brother is.'

Then she dashed from the parlour, no doubt in search of her restored companion.

Thomas did not dash anywhere but stood where he was, wondering what she'd meant by him ending up happy—fearing more than wondering.

There was a price to be paid for happiness, which he was not willing to pay.

Being content would suit him far better.

The last time Evie was required to chaperone she had not been in love with Thomas. Then, she had been concerned for her good friend, worried he would make a mistake in his choice of a bride.

Now, she was still concerned he would. Only her reason for it was far different. Simply said, she did not wish to see him with someone else. She could hardly admit that she loved him. There was no chance what-

soever that he would return her feelings. If there ever
had been, she'd crushed the possibility by misrepre-
senting who she was.

The situation she had landed in was no one's fault
but her own. As uncomfortable as this was, she must
simply bear up.

This would be easier to do if Minerva were here in
the conservatory with her. Watching Thomas and Lydia
sitting at the table enjoying lunch together while she sat
an appropriate distance away, pretending to be absorbed
in a book, was awful—utter misery, in fact. Bearing up
was proving to be more difficult than she'd imagined.

The oddest part was that she was not jealous of his
affections being bestowed on another woman because
they were not. Thomas's affection was motivated by
duty. Which was not to say she was not jealous. She
was positively green with envy that he put devotion
to duty over his own heart. And hers... But to be fair,
he did not know he was doing that. She would need to
tell him she loved him in order for that to be the case.

Looking up from her book, she glanced at Lydia. She
did not appear aglow over having lunch with Thomas.
Surely she wanted more from marriage than Thomas
was willing to give. She deserved more than that.

From where Evie sat, present but not involved...sup-
posedly, she could hear their conversation. They began
by speaking of the weather, then last night's dinner
party at someone's townhouse. Evie had not attended
but Minerva had reported it to be tedious. Then the
conversation turned to the latest fashions arriving from
Paris.

If Thomas did not fall asleep over his soup, she

thought, it would be a wonder. Within five minutes he was bound to be nodding off and she, the dedicated chaperone, along with him. She nearly giggled at the image it presented, but laughing would be more embarrassing than nodding off.

At last the conversation turned to an interesting topic. Smiling, Thomas told Lydia that only three of the parrots had not found homes. She told him she was glad because there would not be as much noise.

And that ended the conversation, as well as Thomas's genuine smile.

What a shame. If it had been Evie she would have kept the conversation going just to see that smile. Did Lydia even recognise how handsome Thomas was when he smiled?

Even when he did not? My stars, but he was exceptionally attractive even when he was scowling.

He was too much of a proper gentleman to let that emotion show, but she thought he must be disturbed at her uncaring attitude. The welfare of the birds was important to him.

Her very dear, quite loved…friend—she must get used to that fact as that was all he would ever be—was making a huge mistake.

Not that he would believe her if she pointed it out. His mind was set and there was nothing she could do about it.

Please, please, please, do not let her sigh her frustration aloud.

Oh, dear, she must have because Thomas glanced suddenly over at her.

What was that expression she saw in his eyes before

he shifted his attention back to his lunch companion? Whatever it was, it had come and gone so quickly that she could not know for certain.

Which did not mean she did not feel it. The unspoken message happened so quickly that she might have imagined it.

Might have, but had not.

Thomas yearned for what they used to have between them. He missed laughing, imaginary battles in the cemetery and kisses—a real one and a near one.

Not that he was likely to ever admit to such in words. But many things were said without words.

What, she wondered, had he seen in her eyes during their wordless exchange?

She was not likely to find out since they had not had a private word since she'd returned to Rivenhall.

He avoided her as much as he could. She avoided him as much as she could. This was an untenable situation and she did not know how much longer it could go on without...

Well, she was not exactly sure what. But she feared it.

She was not meant for him. Anything she did to make him think so would be inappropriate.

In his steady Thomas way he had not met with Lydia's father. As far as Evie could tell from looking at Lydia, he had not told her he intended to do so. But surely she must guess what was coming. Eventually, Thomas would pay that visit and what would Evie do? Smile and wish him well while choking back her tears?

How horribly wrong it was for Thomas to be choosing a woman who did not love him over one who did.

It struck Evie as a sad thing. Lydia was a nice person, kind and polite to everyone she met. The poor woman deserved more than she was going to get from Thomas. She was a victim of old ideas. Ideas that in the end would make her unhappy.

Thanks to her father, Evie was not bound by outdated nonsense. Which did not mean she was not bound. She had admitted to herself that she loved Thomas and that admission must remain a prisoner in her heart. Until the day he recognised that love was the reason to marry, it would remain unspoken.

Hopefully that day would come before it was too late.

'Miss Clarke? Would you be so kind as to accompany us on a walk in the garden?' Thomas asked.

'Yes, I would be delighted to.'

Lies upon lies. She wondered if she would ever find the courage to tell the truth again.

Outside, a brisk breeze freshened the air. She lifted her nose, breathed it in.

While walking a discreet distance behind Thomas and Lydia, the wind caught the hem of her gown and tossed it playfully about. She smiled, feeling the tension wash away. She was not going to miss the beauty of this autumn day due to stress.

In fact, she thought, it might be an insult to dwell on worries in the midst of such beauty. If Lydia was unhappy with her skirt whipping about and her hair coming loose to tickle her face, it was not Evie's concern. In spite of her situation, Evie was going to find her joy, make the choice to live in it.

She shook her head, helping her curls come free. In spite of Mr Glum and his unhappy companion, she found delight in the lovely garden.

* * *

It was quite late and dark when Thomas came home from an evening at his club. While it was not raining yet, heavy clouds pressed the sky.

His driver opened the carriage door. Thomas stepped down to the pavement at the same time that lightning crackled across the sky.

In the instant of the flash he spotted a man standing across the street.

Now, that was odd. However, this was London and odd things did happen at night. Not so often in this part of town, but crime was not unheard of here.

Thunder rumbled. The storm let loose in a downpour.

'Did you see him?' Thomas had to shout to the driver over the racket of rain pelting the street.

'No, sir. My back was turned.' The driver cast a glance over his shoulder. 'No one is there now.'

The rain grew heavier by the second. Water was quickly rising in the kerbs.

He bade the driver goodnight then hurried towards the front door.

Someone had been there and he had been looking at Rivenhall. Given the weather, it was not a prime night for thievery, so what then?

Perhaps it had been as simple as a fellow out walking, his attention drawn to the carriage.

Rushing inside, he put the matter behind him for now.

At this hour the house was quiet. Even his valet would be abed. Expecting to be late, Thomas had given him the night off. He was capable of getting undressed on his own when the need arose.

His brother no longer employed a valet. It must have been a difficult adjustment for William to go from gentleman of the town to sheep farmer. Transformed in a heartbeat from society's rascal to farmer and a husband, or so it seemed. How had he managed? Evie would tell him it was because William was in love and so it would not have been a sacrifice.

Perhaps it was because William was more adaptable than Thomas. That and the fact that, as second son, his brother was not bound by what society expected of him.

Even though Thomas had never dreamed he would envy his brother, there was something nipping at his emotions. It was puzzling. Was it possible that he wanted more of marriage than he'd always believed? Seeing William and Elizabeth together always left him with a smile.

He would have his time to smile once he resolved things with Lydia. In a few weeks' time it would be appropriate to speak with her father. Yes, then he would smile. Perhaps it would not be for the same reason William did, but a goal accomplished, a duty seen to, was something to feel good about.

The hour was late and he was weary. Still, he did not believe he would be able to sleep. He decided to spend some time in the small parlour, watching out of the window for a while to see if the mysterious voyeur returned.

The parlour door was closed. The space between the frame and the door was illuminated in a soft orange glow. There must be a fire in the hearth.

That was odd. The staff were diligent about banking the flames before bed. It was unlikely that anyone was awake this late.

But then, what was one more odd occurrence to-night?

He drew the door open and caught his breath on a gasp. No one was awake, but someone was in the room…sleeping.

Evie lay on the couch with a book open across her chest. It moved up and down with her steady breathing. The red ribbon tying the gown closed at her throat ruffled with her breath.

He took a step backward. It was not proper to be watching her sleep.

But then she smiled and he forgot propriety…who he was and who she was.

One hand lay against her cheek. Her fingers caught a wisp of curling red hair. It looked as if she was blushing, but that might have to do with the reflection of flames on her skin.

Leaning against the door frame, arms crossed over his chest, he wondered what she was dreaming about.

Something happy—no one could look that way during a nightmare.

The vision she presented made him smile even though he had no idea what was making her lips curve in such a sweet way.

But then, maybe not sweet so much as seductive.

Then it occurred to him that she might be dreaming about her fiancé and his smile fled. The rest of him ought to flee as well.

Ought to, but quite against his will, he felt riveted to the spot. Very well, it might not be against his will but it was against good reason.

Good reason was the guiding principle of his life.

Because it was, he ought to climb the stairs and lock himself in his chamber. Lock temptation out.

The problem was, visions of Evie, sweetly yet seductively reclining on the couch, would march through the wooden door.

'You are making me question everything,' he whispered.

Hearing his own voice saying so snapped him out of the trance she had bound him in. He did not wish to question anything. His life was fine as it was.

When his father returned he would find his firstborn doing what he had been raised to do since boyhood—overseeing the well-being of Rivenhall.

He was not his brother. William was, and always had been, free to please himself. Thomas's position in the family was the same as it had always been. It would not change. As firstborn, how could it? He was simply not free to follow his own desires. The estate would always come first.

If his father could see him staring at the lady on the couch, a member of the household under his care, if he could sense Thomas's dedication to Rivenhall wavering, he would be distressed.

Straightening, he walked backwards quietly, closing the parlour door behind him. No, he was not going to waver, he was not going to distress his father.

Going up the stairs to his chamber, he counted himself a fool. A great fool! What had got into him, staring at Evie for as long as he had? It was going to take some doing to see her as Miss Clarke.

If he meant to be sincere in his courtship of his neighbour, he must put away the manner in which his heart twisted, galloped, by coming upon Evie unexpectedly. She lived in his household and such things would happen. He would need to get used to it.

He closed his chamber door and, as expected, Evie's image marched through.

What her image did next shook him. She took his face between her soft, hot palms and kissed him soundly on the mouth. It shook him because she had not actually marched through his door. His imagination had opened the door, invited her inside. It was his own heart creating and then indulging in the fantasy.

He had set high-principled Thomas aside and given himself over to the Thomas he had once been. The young one who'd laughed freely and often. The one that only Evie seemed to summon from his heart.

It did not matter that he had followed the fantasy for only an instant. He had done it and knocked himself off the high-principled pedestal he had put himself on so many years ago.

It was a tall pedestal and he was not certain he could climb back up.

Worse, he was not certain he wanted to.

And yet, sitting down hard on his bed, watching the rain lash against his chamber window, he started up, hand over hand. He climbed until he imagined his hands bleeding. Unless the blood was not coming from his hands, but from his heart.

In the end it did not matter because he was the future Viscount of Rivenhall.

* * *

Evie gazed out of the parlour window, waiting for the rain to stop. It had pummelled the house relentlessly from the wee hours, then most of the morning.

Having eaten lunch then finished the book she'd fallen asleep reading last night, she needed to go outside and breathe some fresh air.

Even a house as large as Rivenhall could close in upon one when one was forced to spend too much time indoors.

Raindrops slicked the window pane, giving the impression of a waterfall. Nothing of great interest was happening out there.

A carriage passed the house, then someone walked by huddled under an umbrella. Due to the blur on the window she could not say if it was a man or a woman. As interesting things went, watching someone walking in the rain was not one.

What she ought to do was take an umbrella and go outside. She did enjoy walking in the rain, only not this much rain.

Hearing voices from the hallway, she peeped out of the parlour door.

Thomas and Minerva. It appeared that Thomas was going out. She envied him. Perhaps she should run after him and beg to go along, wherever it was he was going. It was bound to be more interesting than staring out of the window.

However, asking to go along would mean speaking to him, which would be awkward since he'd had very little to say to her since bringing her back to Rivenhall.

And why would he wish to speak with her? Not only

had she misrepresented who she was, but Lord Haverly had told him she was engaged.

The Rivenhall carriage pulled up in front of the house. Thomas dashed down the path then climbed inside without waiting for the driver to open the door for him.

Where was he going? To seek an audience with Lydia's father? Perhaps he was. It was bound to happen some time. The sooner she became used to the idea of Thomas and Lydia being engaged, the better. He was never meant to be hers in the first place.

'It is a wonder my brother did not hear you sigh all the way from in here.' Minerva swept into the parlour, grinning.

'Did he?' That would be embarrassing.

'I sneezed or he would have heard.' Minerva joined her at the window. 'But perhaps I should not have. This day is so dreary. Watching Thomas trying not to react to your admiration would have been diverting.'

'Who would not admire him? He is a good and decent man.'

'Actually, William is the one who was admired as a man. Poor Thomas—it's his future title which is admired. Except by you. You are in love with the good person he is.'

How did Minerva know that? She certainly had not learned it from Evie. Except that she'd seen her kissing Thomas, so denying her feelings would be useless.

'It does not matter, does it? Not when he is probably on his way to pay a call on Lydia's father. But please, Minerva. You must not tell him.'

'Naturally, it is not for me to do so. But you must.'

She shook her head. 'He would not wish to know.'

'When it comes to my brother, what he thinks he wants is not what he really does want…certainly not what is best for him.'

'Regardless, wedding Lydia is his choice. If we wish to be free to choose, he should also be free to choose.'

'It is a fair point and yet…he will end up miserable.'

'Even though I agree, there is nothing we can do about it. He might very well return home with an agreement made between him and Lord Brownton.'

'He did not go to visit Lord Brownton. He went to visit the constable. It seems that someone was staring at the house late last night. My brother has a bad feeling about it.'

'Who would be doing that?'

But she had an idea who—the possibility made her heart crash against her ribs. Oh, please let it be someone else. It simply could not be Cousin Hubert. It was too horrible to consider.

'Thomas was not even sure the person was watching Rivenhall.'

'Certain enough to visit the constable.'

'Crime is uncommon here, but not unheard of… Why are your hands shaking?' Minerva frowned at her. 'Tell me about this fiancé of yours.'

'My hands are shaking because it is cold in here. And I never had a fiancé. Lord Haverly was mistaken.'

'All right, Evie. You have your secrets and I respect that. I shall not press you on them…but I shall wonder.'

'I am weary of staring out of this window, waiting for something to happen. Don't we have any social calls to pay?'

'Not today. We can attempt to teach Charm a trick, if you like,' Minerva answered.

'Splendid. Let me gather her up and we will see what comes of it.'

Chapter Fourteen

Evie knew that Thomas had returned two hours ago and, as far as she knew, had not mentioned what had come of his visit to the constable. She had been listening to the conversations of others since she was not likely to hear anything from him. He was avoiding her company more studiously than he had before. As if such a thing were even possible. When they passed in a hallway he nodded without engaging her eyes or, if he could manage, did not even nod. It was hard to imagine what she had done to make him even more distant.

If she could, she would waylay him on the stairs or in a hallway and ask what he had discovered about the person who might or might not have been watching the house. Since she did not wish to alert him to the fact that she was concerned, she kept the worry to herself. Somewhat to herself. It was clear that Minerva knew she was worried.

At least the storm was moving away. If she wished, she could grab an umbrella and go outside. Yet, as tempting as it was, she did not dare. Not until there was word about who had been standing in the rain last night. She might never know who the stranger was, but until some time passed without his return she would stay inside where it was safe. She would keep watch at the parlour window…continue to, as it were.

A bright golden line of sunset sky divided the lifting storm from the horizon. It was a dramatic scene, so cold and beautiful. With light reflecting off the pavement it looked as if diamonds had been scattered on the surface.

It was such a spectacular show that she failed at first to see the man standing on the pavement. But there he was. She could not see his face, the fading light was at his back, but she recognised the lazy stance of his posture.

How had he got there? Not by carriage. The nearest one she could see was all the way down at the park, making a turn into the entrance.

A quick rage filled her. How dared he come here? Did he imagine she would go back with him?

It was a lucky thing she was alone or someone would see her hands curled into fists, shaking against her best efforts to control them. It would not be wise to go outside and confront him—possibly the worst thing she could do, other than allow him to approach the front door.

If he brought his selfish, underhanded, miserable demands to Rivenhall's door she could not bear it. For him to come inside, present himself as her poor wounded relative who only sought her best interests would be… It made her angry to think of it.

Oh, no…this was not going to happen!

He stood quite still, just staring at the house. She

wondered why he did not reach for the gate if he meant to approach. But he was a coward so he might be worried that the people living here knew the truth about him.

Now she wished they did.

No matter, she was going out. He was alone and if he got too close she would scream. There was every chance that Minerva was looking out of an upstairs window at this very moment.

Without bothering to take her coat, she hurried down the front steps. The pavement was still slick so she had to pick her way along rather than rush after Hubert in the fit of rage she felt pulsing through her.

How dared he come here?

'Thomas! Thomas!'

He heard Minerva screeching his name while he sat on the edge of the bed taking off his boots, rolling off his socks to change for dinner.

Lurching to his feet, he ran barefoot towards his chamber door. His sister never screeched.

The door burst open before he touched it.

'Evie is being kidnapped!'

That made no sense but—

'Where?' he asked, already on a run down the hallway.

'In front!' He heard his sister's footsteps racing down the stairs behind him. She was calling something out, but he did not know what.

He discovered when he burst out of the house.

Three men, one of them old, stoop-shouldered and

dressed as a gentleman, were yanking and pulling on Evie, trying to force her into a carriage.

She kicked and screamed. A seam of her gown ripped at the shoulder.

One of the men, a burly young thug, snatched her around the waist and lifted her off the pavement. He covered her mouth with his hand. Evie swung her legs madly. All of a sudden he yelped.

Good, she must have bitten him.

The man waved his hand as if to shake off the pain. Then curled it into a fist.

Being barefoot put Thomas at a disadvantage. Cold, hard fury gave him an edge. Also, the man was so intent on hurting Evie he did not seem to notice Thomas.

Leading with his shoulder, he ploughed into the thug, hitting him in the small of his back.

In the second the thug let go of Evie in an attempt to recover from his fall, Thomas grabbed her around the shoulders, clutching her to himself so that if the man rolling on the ground tried to snatch her again he would grab nothing but air.

'Get up!' the old man yelled. 'Do what you were paid to do!'

Paid? What the blazes was going on here?

When the grounded man continued to curl into himself and moan, the old man gave him a kick in the behind.

'You promised me a bride, Dumel!' he shouted at the third man. 'Get her!'

This was the fiancé? A debauched-looking old goat?

The round, middle-aged man being shouted at had

been hanging back, watching the fight while also staring evil-eyed murder at Evie.

'Come along, Violet.' The round one's voice trembled with anger. 'Ada and I are finished with your nonsense. It is a wonder Baron Falcon still wants you after the stunt you pulled.'

'No, Hubert.' Evie's voice trembled while she clung to the lapels of Thomas's coat, shaking her head. He drew her tighter to him because she was shivering as if she would fall apart.

'It's all right. You are safe,' he said as soothingly as he was able.

'Sir, I insist that you hand my relative over to me. She has not been herself lately and we fear for her mental state. Womanly hysteria, you understand. She needs the firm hand of a husband to keep her—'

Suddenly, the fellow who claimed to be the relative roared in pain.

In the disturbance no one had noticed Minerva coming outside. Although he ought to have known she would. Also that she would come out armed. It was only an umbrella, but it had a wickedly pointed end, which she'd used to whack the kidnapper in a delicate place.

'If you are referring to my fiancée,' Thomas said deliberately, making sure the point he made was as sharp as the one on Minerva's umbrella, 'I promise you, you shall not have her.'

Evie went quite still in his arms.

'This is nonsense,' said the old man. 'You were mine first. Get in the coach, girl. I will not tolerate disobedience in a bride.'

Thomas loosened his grip on Evie's shoulder, but

only to make it appear she could go to the villain if she wished to. At the same time he kept her close enough to prevent her from doing so.

'Miss Dumel,' he said, taking half a step away only. 'I understand how important choice is to you. Which one of us are you betrothed to? Do you choose him, or do you choose me?'

For a moment Evie stared at Thomas, stunned.

She knew what he'd said, but the words did not settle in her brain at first.

'I choose you, Thomas,' she half stuttered.

Because what woman with a beating heart, a rapidly beating heart, would not?

In the moment he was her safe haven. She did not dare to even let go of his coat. She understood he did not mean it. This was his way of protecting her from her abductors.

One of whom still lay on the wet street too afraid to rise. For good reason, since the tip of Minerva's circling umbrella was only inches from his nose.

This was now the second time Thomas had snatched her from the hands of a wicked man. How could she not fall in love with her hero all over again?

She understood this was a ruse on Thomas's part but for just a moment she let her heart melt. If only saying 'I choose you, Thomas' meant she actually was choosing him.

'See here! Send her across to me at once,' Hubert demanded.

'The lady has made her choice.' She felt the rumble of Thomas's words when he drew her tightly to him.

She had never realised the circle of a man's arms, the deep, commanding tone of his voice could be sanctuary. But here she was, feeling safe in the midst of danger.

'The lady does not have a choice.' Hubert had a nasty scowl which made the corners of his mouth turn down and his pointed nose almost touch his upper lip. 'I have a contract which gives Violet's hand in marriage to Baron Falcon.'

'A lady always has a choice,' Thomas answered.

What was that? A cheer—from Minerva.

'You may expect a visit from my lawyer within the week,' Hubert spat. 'We will see how much the chit's choice counts against what her guardian decides. As I said, she is hysterical and not able to decide anything for herself. If she refuses to wed this good and decent man, I am afraid it is the asylum for her...until she understands what is best for her.'

She should not be afraid. But, as her closest male relative, would he really be able to commit her to an institution for hysteria? She had heard of such things happening to perfectly sane women.

Were it not for Thomas's arms closed protectively about her, she might weep or faint. But they were around her and she knew nothing could harm her as long as she stood where she was.

Which was not something she could do for ever. Very soon she must leave Rivenhall again. Hubert might not succeed in having her put away, but it was not a risk she could take.

'Come, my sweet,' Thomas said, then waved at his sister to follow. 'We are finished here.'

How did he expect her legs to work properly after

he'd called her 'my sweet'? It was not as if he meant it. Saying those words had been to deceive Hubert and nothing more. She reminded herself that she was not 'his sweet', nor was she his fiancée. It was only that she lived in his home and was under his care. He would protect anyone who lived here.

Thomas led them inside, closing the door on bellows of rage and cursing coming from the street.

The butler waited in the foyer, along with a few of the staff, all of them looking alarmed.

Thomas dropped his arms from about her, giving a sharp nod to the butler.

'Mr Hooper. Please summon my solicitor. Tell him I will require a special licence no later than three days from now.'

What was that?

'A special licence…as in regard to marriage?' Minerva asked, her mouth a perfect circle of surprise.

'I can scarcely wed Evie without one.'

What? What? Her mind seemed stuck. No…she could not have heard that.

Except that she must have since Mr Hooper nodded and said, 'As you wish, sir.'

'No, Mr Hooper!' she called. 'That will not be necessary.'

'See to it, Hooper.' Thomas settled his gaze on her, his expression severe.

'I realise that you did not mean it,' she told him. 'You need not follow through with it.'

'I asked who you chose. You chose me.'

He walked towards the stairway. She ran after him, tugging hard on the back of his coat. It was then that she noticed his bare feet. Thomas had run to her rescue barefoot. That touched her as much as anything had in the last quarter of an hour. Even so, she could not possibly go along with this since it was clear that he had lost his mind. The drama of the evening had got to him.

'But, Thomas. You do not want to marry me.'

The oddest expression shadowed his eyes, there and gone in a second. She might have felt the meaning of it if she were not too stunned to feel anything. And yet there was something nipping at her heart. She tapped her mouth with her finger, the floor with her toe, trying to identify what it was.

Confusion. Yes, that summed it up well.

But Thomas did not seem confused, only determined.

'That is neither here nor there. We will wed. Or do you prefer to be sent to an institution?'

'No, but—'

'Minnie,' he said, cutting off her argument, 'may I trust you to do whatever is necessary to arrange a wedding ceremony?'

'Of course. I shall delight in it. As long as this is what our Evie wishes.' Minerva turned her attention from her brother to Evie. 'Do you wish it?'

More than anything. But not under these circumstances. She could not possibly marry the man she loved without him loving her too.

'Under the circumstances, it does not matter if she wishes it or not.'

Thomas was such a viscount…so determined and in charge. She had never met Thomas's father, but she imagined he would be proud of this attitude, if not of the woman his son was insisting upon marrying. As Evie understood it, Lord Rivenhall had his heart set on Thomas wedding Lydia, a born and bred viscount's daughter.

While Evie was also a lady of society, her rank was not as sought after. Which mattered for nothing when it came to matters of the heart.

In no way was Thomas proposing a matter of the heart. How could she hope they might have a loving marriage?

'Evie still needs to say what she thinks, Thomas. Only moments ago you said that a lady has a choice.' Minerva gave her brother a smile which made him blink, then frown even more deeply.

'If I can go through with this, so can Evie.'

'Evie would rather end her days a shrivelled old spinster,' Evie exclaimed, inserting her sentiment into the conversation because whose opinion mattered more?

'Ah, but "shrivelled old spinster" is not among your choices.' He folded his arms across his chest, bent slightly at the waist, and peered at her with an arch look. 'As I recall it, your choices are to wed the old goat, be sent to an institution until you wed the old goat, or to wed me.'

'The young goat?' Minerva grinned.

'If you wish,' he answered, casting his sister a frown. 'But however you see me, this situation is not something to jest about. Evie's future is in peril. I see no solution but for us to wed.'

Solution? It was crushing to know that was how he would see their marriage. She was a problem to be dealt with, not a wife to be loved.

Not a woman he had kissed, who had held his heart for a moment in time. A woman whose heart he had held ever since.

She stepped away from him and Minerva, staring at the rug, at the chair leg and the umbrella beside the doorway.

Thomas was correct. She had no choice in what was about to happen. It did not matter how deeply she wanted a love match, it was not going to happen for her.

For all that she needed to give Thomas an answer… Although he was not asking for an answer so much as acknowledgement of his decision. She needed to speak up, or at least to nod, but she simply could not.

'Give us a moment, will you, Minnie?' Thomas's voice softened from the demanding tone he had been using.

Walking past her, Minerva paused and whispered in her ear. 'My brother is right, you know. You must marry him.'

Had anyone but Minerva said that she would have dismissed it out of hand, but she and her friend were of like mind when it came to marriage.

Seconds later she heard Thomas coming towards her, his long bare feet softly slapping the floor.

'I do not know what I should call you.' It seemed as if he was standing close. The rush of his breath stirred the loose curls on top of her head.

'Oh, Violet, I suppose. I have gone by it all of my life. But Evie is also my name if you would rather use that.'

'I know very well that marrying me is not what you wish.' How could he know what she wished when she herself did not know? In other circumstances there was nothing she would wish for more than to marry this man. 'But surely you can see the need for it?'

If Hubert actually could connive to have her put away, then yes, she did see the need.

Slowly turning, she looked up at his face. It should not come as a surprise to see that his eyes seemed dark and troubled. If they wed she was not the only one who would give something up.

'What about Lydia? She is the one you want to marry.' What kind of person was she? One she did not like overmuch in the moment. She had intentionally deceived Thomas and was now probably going to break another woman's heart. 'I imagine she is on pins waiting for you to declare your intentions,' she said.

'I rather doubt that. She will not lack suitors.'

'But your father—'

'Is in Scotland and not involved in this.'

He was dismissing her arguments rather neatly. But at what cost to himself? Pleasing his father was important to him. She believed it was the primary reason he'd intended to court Lydia. Ever responsible, ever above reproach, Thomas must feel he would be letting his father down by wedding Evie.

'You are giving up too much, Thomas. I cannot let you do it.'

The moment stretched, long and uncomfortable, while they looked at one another.

Thomas spoke first. 'It is time to make your choice.'

Make a choice which she did not have.

Thomas had one, though. He could place her valise outside the front door and send her on her way. He was not obliged to stand up for her.

And yet he was.

Very well. 'You asked what you should call me. Mrs Grant…call me that, Thomas.'

'Good then. I will see you at dinner.'

Bare feet slapping the cold floor, he strode out of the foyer…and ever deeper into her heart.

It occurred to her while she stood alone, glancing about the elegant Rivenhall foyer, she did have half of what she'd dreamed of in marriage.

She would be marrying a man she loved, if not one who loved her.

He was betrothed. Two hours ago Thomas had been considering his courtship of his neighbour and now he was wondering if he needed to even inform her that everything had changed.

The courtship between them had barely taken the first step. Lydia would be surprised when she discovered he was suddenly married but not heartbroken. At worst she would be disappointed. And not because of losing him, but rather losing the opportunity to one day become Viscountess Rivenhall.

His father would suffer more disappointment than anyone.

Dinner was proving to be an awkward, silent affair, with everyone absorbed in their own thoughts. The staff, standing by, seemed highly curious about what was going on. Word would have spread that the future Viscount had lost his mind, done something so out of character that they must be wondering who he was.

He could hardly blame them for it because even he was wondering who he was…what had got into him, proposing marriage…no, not proposing so much as demanding.

Glancing down the table, he wondered what his future bride was thinking. The way she lifted her spoon to her lips in a regular rhythm, her eyes trained on the soup bowl, he could not tell.

Sitting here at the table, he was not likely to find out.

He stood up. 'Evie, will you meet me at the aviary when you have finished dining?'

Setting her spoon aside, she stood up. 'I am finished. Shall we walk there together?'

With a nod at a footman, he indicated that their coats should be brought.

There were things he wanted to ask her and he could not do it here with people listening.

Even bundled in coats the night was cold so he set a quick pace to the conservatory. Once inside he lit the stove closest to the aviary, which was built so that it was partly inside the conservatory and partly in the garden, giving the birds freedom to be inside when the weather was cold and outside when the sun was bright and warm. Thomas was proud of the structure. But he did wonder what his father would think of the changes he'd made, knowing the conservatory had always been a special place for his parents.

More than the changes he'd made to the conservatory, he wondered how well his father would accept the decisions he'd made affecting Rivenhall's future.

Choosing the new Lady Rivenhall was something to be done with great thought and much deliberation—a matter of such importance that he and his father would talk it over at length before any decisions were reached.

In claiming Evie, he had given the matter no thought, no deliberation. As far as discussing it with his father... well, he would be married well before his father returned from Scotland.

Outrage had made Thomas act in the moment. Now that he was no longer outraged, he had time to wonder if he might have done it differently.

'You went to a great deal of effort and expense to take care of these birds, Thomas.' Standing close to the stove, Evie shrugged out of her coat and set it on a bench. 'Do you always give so much of yourself to help the helpless?'

'I do not know what you mean. The parrots needed a shelter and I had one built.'

'I was speaking of how you are helping me. Truly, it is above and beyond your duty.'

She made him sound far nobler than he was. He had been angry seeing those men with their hands on her, her gown torn at the shoulder. He had spoken in passion.

It had not been reason and logic that had made him charge barefoot out of the house. He had acted from his heart. Something he never did.

However, this was not the moment to explore why.

He'd brought her out here for a reason, to have a question answered. He could not consider anything else until he had an answer.

'Evie—' He was glad she did not wish to be called Violet. He did not know Miss Violet Dumel. Perhaps she was the same woman, no matter the name. He liked the Evie he had come to know. They had been friends only a short time ago, great friends.

'What is it, Thomas?' He must have been silent for

too long while he searched her expression, looking for the lady he had known.

'Shall we sit? I need to ask you something.'

'I can only imagine what.' She gave a great sigh then plopped down on the bench. 'Ask away, Thomas.'

All right, this was something Evie would say. In spite of his sombre mood something stirred—a small tickle in his heart.

'Why did the Baron, your cousin, believe you were engaged? Did you agree to it and then back out? What I want to know is if you have any kind of obligation to Falcon?' Lawyers had been threatened. He needed to know what he was up against. Not that he was going to change his mind, but still, he did need to know. 'Did you agree to marry that man?'

A tremble took her. She rubbed her arms briskly. He doubted it was because of the cold night since the stove provided adequate heat. 'I did not agree to marry him. I did not refuse either, at least within my cousin's hearing.'

'You might not be where you are now had you done so.'

'What I would be is married to Baron Falcon. No... Thomas, I could not protest or my cousin would have taken steps to prevent me from leaving. On the night before the Baron came to propose, I ran away from home. I think you know me well enough to know I would never accept a proposal which was not made in love—'

Her gaze away from him. She bit her bottom lip.

'And yet you will marry me.'

And then, to his utter surprise, she smiled. It caught him off guard, gave his heart a hard kick.

'In this case I will make an exception.'

She looked at him full-on. Her beautiful eyes seemed to be probing his heart. 'Do you believe me? I have told you the truth.'

Did he? She had deceived him before. Baron Gossmere had come for her so he must have thought he was justified in it.

'Very well, if you believe my cousin you do not know me.' She stood up and snatched her coat, her smile gone. 'Until you can see past Hubert's treachery, until you see me, we have nothing else to say... We cannot go on from here.' She shrugged one arm into her coat.

No, she could not leave now. They had only begun to speak on what was important.

Standing, he caught her free hand. 'I am sorry. Won't you stay? I will do my best not to behave as a goat.'

She smiled Evie's smile, took off her coat then sat back down.

'Tell me, Evie, how did you manage it? From what you tell me, I assume it was a risky thing to do.' From what he was learning of Evie's cousin, he was a disreputable brute. He hated the thought that she'd ever lived under the same roof with him. 'Did he ever...ever hurt you? You may tell me anything. It won't make a difference in my promise to wed you.'

'Promise, was it? Thomas, someone needs to teach you the difference between a promise and a threat.' Oddly enough, her voice was not accusing when she said it. A humorous glint played in her eyes.

'I have no doubt that between you and my sister I will learn things I never knew I needed to learn.'

'But, as to your question...no, he never hurt me. I

was his greatest asset. He stood to be paid a good sum of money from Baron Falcon for me.'

'I am relieved to hear it. I would not wish to lay the man flat for accosting my wife.'

His wife? He had called her that so casually, with such warmth, it startled him.

It made him look at her in a way he had never looked at Lydia. That was odd, since he had been thinking of wedding his neighbour for much longer than the few hours he had been determined to wed Evie.

'That would make it three times you pummelled a man in my defence. Will you make a habit of it, I wonder?'

'I pray that I will not need to.'

But he would. Clearly, he had a strong need to protect this woman.

He had never felt this way before. It was puzzling, left him wondering—had he in some way sensed she was his to watch over even from the start? Was it possible that his heart had been leaning towards Evie all along and him not aware of it?

Perhaps time had nothing to do with what was in his heart. And what, exactly was in his heart? He did not know. What he did know was that all of a sudden the future held a glimmer of promise.

Thomas's gaze settled upon her. She thought he looked confused.

She had held nothing back from him, except for the most important thing. He could not possibly be guessing that in her moment of honesty she had been dishonest.

Not dishonest in anything she had done or said.

Only in what she had not told him. But truly, she did not think he would appreciate a declaration of true love. If the time came that she could admit her feelings for him, it needed to be special…and shared between them.

Sadly, love was not something Thomas required of a marriage. Exposing her feelings to him now would only make for a painfully awkward situation. Love was something he would need to discover on his own, to feel on his own. She could not reveal her heart to him now, but perhaps one day. This hope gave her the courage to go along with his plan to keep her safe.

It was a good plan; she could not argue it was not. Once she was Thomas's wife, there was nothing Cousin Hubert could do to her.

As Mrs Grant, she could even pay a visit to Mary.

As Mrs Grant, she would be allowed to call this large, wonderful home her own. Had she not been drawn to it from the first time she'd walked up the front path?

She might have lost her home at Gossmere, but she would not lose Rivenhall.

Better, she would not lose Thomas. She would live under his roof, see him every day…and every night.

That last thought made her feel rather warm. A flush crept from her chest, up her neck and flared in her cheeks. Hopefully he did not notice, because how was she to explain it without explaining how her heart melted when she imagined having him as her husband. That on her part the marriage was a love match.

By wedding him there was a chance he might come to love her…a chance he would share her love and rejoice in it.

All of a sudden the future held a glimmer of hope.

Chapter Fifteen

Thomas stood in front of the chapel in Mayfair, watching for the Rivenhall carriage to turn the corner.

Dressed in his finest suit, he waited for his bride to arrive, feeling both grateful and guilty.

Grateful that his sister had used her powers of persuasion to secure the use of the chapel at late notice—and that she had made sure it was decorated in flowers and ribbons.

When he had gone inside a few moments ago to meet with the clergyman, he had been greeted first by the organ player, who was rehearsing strains of Wagner's Wedding March. It sounded very grand for only the three of them, the clergyman and his wife.

The future Viscountess Rivenhall did deserve something grand. So far, he'd given her nothing.

This was where he felt guilty. The only things he had done towards this wedding were to arrange for the licence and dress in his best suit.

If Evie took joy in her wedding morning it would be because of Minerva.

His fiancée of three days had not even had a proper proposal. Caught up in the necessity of wedding her quickly, the righteousness of his duty, he had been negligent.

A lout…yes, a goat!

The plod of horses' hooves announced that a carriage was about to turn the corner. The familiar creak of the wheels and the jingle of the tack assured him it was Rivenhall's.

The carriage stopped in front of the church. The driver helped Minerva out first then reached up a hand to help Evie down.

'Wait!' his sister exclaimed. 'Go inside, Thomas. You are not allowed to see her until she enters the church. After that you may weep at the sight of your bride.'

What was she talking about?

'I must speak to my fiancée before we begin. It is important.'

'It is all right, Minerva. I will speak with him.'

'Very well. But do not weep until she is coming down the aisle,' she whispered.

Weep? Was it required? Because he did not believe he could… Then he looked at Evie. His heart took the oddest turn…a giant lump pressed his throat.

The woman descending the carriage steps on the arm of the beaming driver looked more angel than woman, except for her hair, which was mischief come out to play.

Where on earth had his sister found a gown that resembled a heavenly garment? His mind recognised it as silk, lace and satin but his heart saw the dress of an angelic being.

Somehow, an ethereal spirit had agreed to marry him.

Or she would have agreed had he actually asked. It was past time to take care of that.

Hurrying forward, he took her hand, escorted her inside the vestibule of the chapel. The tune the organ was playing made him feel light, his heart expanded. He was about to wed the loveliest woman he had ever seen. He could not, but he feared he might, shed a tear before the appointed time.

This made no sense whatsoever. Theirs was not a love match.

'Evie...' The lump tightened, he blinked twice, glanced anywhere but into her eyes.

'What is it, Thomas?' She touched the buttons on his coat. 'Have you changed your mind?'

'It isn't that.' He caught her hand at the same time he looked at her face, became lost in what he saw in her eyes. But no, he could not possibly be seeing that. He was forcing her to wed him—and being forced was the last thing she wanted.

Perhaps he saw what he wanted to see. But no...that was not what he wanted either. Love had never been a consideration for him when it came to marriage.

What then? He had no idea what except that he was doing what he must.

Going down on his knee, he took her hand, steadied his breathing and caught his runaway heart because it was wilfully trying to escape his ribs.

'Violet Evie Dumel, will you do me the honour of becoming my wife?'

She nodded, smiled. 'Yes, Thomas, I will.'

It was a relief to have that done with. A proper proposal was something she deserved. He had fulfilled his duty in that, at least.

Later on tonight he would have another duty to fulfil. He was not certain what he was going to do about it. Or not do, more to the point.

He stood up, kissed her hand, then pressed it to his heart.

'I think we will be all right, my friend,' he told her.

With a nod, he turned and went into the sanctuary.

He took his place beside his sister while they waited for the organ to begin the Wedding March.

'Thomas Grant, I told you to wait until she came down the aisle.'

What? He brushed his cheek with the back of his hand. It came away moist. He had not meant for that to happen, would have informed anyone it was impossible because—

And then the organ music swelled.

Evie came towards him, offering up the rest of her life to his care.

He was not quick enough to catch the tear dripping off the end of his nose, but Minerva was.

Violet stared at her husband's study door, wondering if she ought to knock or enter unannounced.

This was her home now and she should be able to go wherever she wished to, just as Thomas was her husband, and she should be able to waltz into his presence unannounced.

And yet she stood in the hallway feeling shy. A few things had changed in the ten days since she'd wed.

Her name for one. Mrs Thomas Grant... Violet Evie Grant.

Also, the location of her chamber had changed. It was now next to Thomas's chamber. It was as pretty as her old one, but it had clearly been unoccupied since... who knew when? One day soon she would redecorate it to suit her own tastes.

The most interesting feature of the chamber, and one she would not change, was the door which connected it to Thomas's room.

So far it had remained locked, a reminder of the one thing that had not changed with her marriage. She was as pure a maiden as the day she was wed.

She pursed her lips at the closed office door. Nothing was going to change in that area unless she found a key.

Not a key to the adjoining door, she did not mean that, but rather a key to unlock her husband's heart. A key to release his joy.

Lately, he was diligently keeping the fun side of his nature shut away. Until he let it out and let her in, she had no desire for the bedroom door to open. She was not going to share a marriage bed with him unless there was love between them—love declared and celebrated.

Since this was not the case, she found life rather lonely. Minerva had gone north to visit William and Elizabeth, which left her with Charm and a too-busy husband for company.

With the day nearly spent, she was ready to spend time with Thomas who, not untypically, had spent the entire day in his study.

All she needed to do was knock...no, not knock,

rather walk boldly into his cherished space as she had every right to do.

Very well. She turned the knob, pushed the door open.

Thomas was slumped on the blotter of his desk sleeping soundly, his head cradled on his crossed arms. If she wished to engage his company, she would need to wake him.

Not quite yet, though. In a moment, after she'd finished looking at him. Carefully, so he would not wake, she sat down in the chair across the desk from him. She took her time watching him…indulging in the quiet moment. She sighed inside at the way his thick, dark lashes curled up at the ends. They were playful lashes and oh, so handsome. He was frowning deeply, though, seeming distressed.

Perhaps she should not, but she touched his hair, stroking it lightly as if to banish the dream. He wore it short, efficient-looking, as suited his nature and position in the family. Still, it glittered in the lamplight, making it appear as playful as his lashes.

Ah, just there, he smiled in his sleep!

What was he dreaming of? Probably not her, but she was curious to know.

The strands of his hair felt bristly, so interesting under her fingertips, so she kept on stroking. And he kept on smiling.

Thomas was dreaming, but it was not a happy dream. He dreamt that his father had come home and was livid that his eldest son had wed without his consent. He went on and on about how much better a son William was. Thomas tried to remind his father how hard he had worked and did not deserve to be second best, but his mouth was stuck, as if glued by the world's strongest sealing wax.

All at once something changed. It was as if a breeze, or perhaps a breath, stirred his hair. His father vanished, his hurtful attitude replaced with a sense of well-being.

It was smiling that woke him. Or he thought he was awake. Uncertain, he looked across his desk without lifting his head.

He had to be still sleeping since his bride sat across the desk from him, tenderly, gently stroking his hair.

Dreaming, of course he was, because in this state, balanced between being awake and asleep, he thought he caught a glimpse of his mother's face over Evie's shoulder. It was there and gone in an instant, but she had been smiling.

This was a far better dream.

'Ah, you are awake!' Slowly, Evie drew her hand away from his hair.

'I am?' He was?

He sat up, shook the fuzziness from his mind.

'It is a lucky thing. You were dreaming. At first it seemed to be a bad one and then after that a good one.'

'It turns out that the second one was not a dream. Except for the part where my mother was smiling over your shoulder. I am half certain that was a dream.'

'I would like to think she was smiling over my shoulder.'

'She would be. She would like you, Evie.'

He was glad he'd said so because it made Evie smile.

'The other dream was troubling, though?'

Should he tell her? At some point his father would come home and she would have to deal with his ire too. Which did not seem fair. This had been Thomas's doing from the beginning.

'I suppose you should know this now. But Father might not be pleased with our marriage.'

'I assumed he would not be. He did favour Lydia for Rivenhall's Viscountess. But have you heard from him?'

Evie had been there when he'd sent the wire to his father informing him of the marriage. He wondered if she was as nervous as he was about his father's reaction.

After spending a lifetime pleasing the man, his father was bound to be stunned that Thomas had married without consulting him first.

Thomas himself was stunned by what he had done.

However, seeing his bride sitting across from him, her smile finding a spot in his heart, he thought he might not regret it.

'I have come to rescue you, Thomas.'

'Rescue me from what?'

From a bad dream or from the dull marriage he had first thought to have?

'All this.' She indicated his study with a sweep of her hand. 'It is time to have some fun.'

'I did not realise I was not having fun.' Keeping Rivenhall running smoothly might not be fun in her eyes, but it was satisfying.

'Very well, I need to have some fun. There is no one else I might have it with other than you.'

He thought for a moment. What could he do to keep her entertained? A way did present itself which involved fewer clothes, heat and…but no.

Evie deserved more than he could give her in that way. Which shamed him because if he did not offer her love…she would not have it. He was her husband. He should be acting like a husband.

However, no one knew better than he did that she would not accept affection offered out of obligation.

'Not the circus…' he thought out loud.

'Oh, but we do not have any pink dogs so—'

'Not the circus,' he repeated more firmly. 'The theatre?'

'Hmm… That did not work out for the best last time. What if we come home with monkeys?' Luckily she laughed, because…no monkeys. 'Let's take a sunset walk in the park. If we come across a lonely squirrel or two, it should suffice.'

'You don't mind that it's cold and windy?'

She laughed, stood up and reached her hand towards him across the desktop. 'You know I adore wind.'

He did know it. Why did it make him happy knowing small things about her?

Perhaps because she was his…because he'd never expected to know small, personal things about a woman. The marriage he had envisaged, what he'd believed he wanted, did not involve walks in the park on windy afternoons.

Nor did it involve his wife reaching across the desk to take his hand.

The marriage he'd always expected involved shared social events in the public eye. Then, once at home, separate yet friendly lives. Living side by side only, rather like a parallel existence.

Standing, he took Evie's hand then eased out from

around the table. There was no parallel with this woman, there was only entwined.

He was not certain how he felt about an outing…but he was going for a walk.

With his pretty wife who enjoyed the wind.

Evie had one goal in mind. To make Thomas laugh. Somehow she was going to find something to amuse him while they walked.

Entering the park, she spotted several people out enjoying the late autumn afternoon. The wind friskily grabbed skirts and playfully tipped gentlemen's hats.

One fellow cried out, waving his arms while chasing his runaway hat across the grass. This was funny. Glancing sideways at Thomas, he showed no sign of appreciating it. He probably hadn't noticed since his attention was occupied with some of the people walking past and casting them curious looks.

They had not attended a social event since their marriage and Thomas had not made a formal announcement yet. Which was not to say the news was not known by society. Nothing spread more quickly than scandal.

The people they met smiled pleasantly, but with great curiosity about the gossip which was being whispered about.

Oh, my word! It only now occurred to her that they were probably wondering if she was a compromised woman and Thomas to blame. What other reason could there be for such a hasty marriage?

Please, oh, please, do not let the Viscount believe this to be the case. But surely he knew his son well enough to know he was more honourable than that.

Glancing sideways at Thomas, she saw his smile looking tight.

It wounded her deeply to think that anyone would see their marriage as tainted. Her husband had lived an exemplary life in an attempt to make up for the raised brows caused by William and Minerva. It was not fair for such a noble-hearted man as her husband to be looked at suspiciously.

She slipped her arm through his, watched as couple after couple passed by without wishing them well on their new marriage. One old woman actually stared at Evie's waistline as if a child was going to swell in her belly while she gawked. All right, that was almost funny, but she was certain Thomas would not think so.

For his sake she prayed someone would congratulate them on their sudden marriage.

And then, just like that, her prayer was answered and in the most unexpected manner. Lydia and a young man, along with her chaperone, sat on a bench beside a fountain when Evie and Thomas passed by.

Seeing them, Lydia rose from her conversation then hurried towards them.

'I have heard the news!' she exclaimed, but in her refined way. 'How wonderful.'

'I fear I owe you an apology,' Thomas said, looking sheepish.

He was spared having to grovel while offering it when Lydia waved her hand in dismissal. 'I am surprised it took you so long to recognise where your heart belonged,' she said to Thomas, but her smile was settled on Evie. When Thomas looked confused she added, 'I noticed the way you looked at Evie in the garden that night when she served as our chaperone.'

Surprised, Evie raised her brows at Thomas. He raised his back at her. Lydia had seen much more than she'd imagined.

'I wish you every happiness.' She squeezed Evie's hands then released them. 'I must return to my friends.'

The exchange had taken only a moment, but it had attracted the attention of other visitors to the park.

Having received the blessing of such a respected young lady, others began to offer their good wishes.

Evie felt it when Thomas's mood began to lift.

But soon they were the only ones remaining in the park. She was going to make him have fun, perhaps even laugh out loud.

'I challenge you to a race.' There was nothing like a good competition. Everyone loved a race.

'Here?' Very well, not everyone.

'Not here.' She pointed to the path at their feet, then circled her arm to encompass the empty park. 'Here.'

'Is there a prize?'

'Of course. There must be a prize. It will be determined by the winner, so you must do what you can to win.'

He looked her over, a slow grin spreading on his face. One brow lifted, giving him the appearance of pure mischief. 'You have the disadvantage of your skirt.'

'Which will make my win all the sweeter, Thomas.' He laughed, and she melted inside. Having wobbly legs put her at more of a disadvantage than her skirts did. However, if her goal was to let out his joy she was already a winner. 'Here is our course. It is three times around that fountain, then across that long stretch of grass. After that we will weave in and out of those trees, back across the grass and then for the hardest part. Do you see those three benches? We shall run across the top of each one. Since we will be winded by then it will be difficult. And we must accomplish all three without falling off. If we do, it means we must do it over again. Not the whole race, only the benches.'

'Is that it?'

Please, yes…she was already winded just thinking about it. 'Well, of course you must beat me back to this spot.'

He bent to kiss her cheek. 'Let's go!'

With a wink, off he went. He was a long stride in front before she gathered her skirts and tucked them into the hem of her waistband.

Clearly he had cheated! And he'd done it with a wink. How absolutely marvellous. This had to be young Thomas come to play.

Laughing, running hard, she overtook him going around the fountain, but he pulled ahead crossing the grass. More agile than he was, she gained the lead, weaving among the trees.

'Ha!' she shouted over her shoulder.

But her lead only lasted a few seconds because, once in the open again, she felt a drag on the back of her skirt. She slapped at Thomas's hand where it was closed in the fabric, pulling her backwards.

'Cheat!' she called, but he passed her by.

When they got to the benches she caught up for a moment because he was struggling with the up and down.

Oh, curses, she was no better at it.

Up they went, down they fell, up…down, laughing constantly. It was a lucky thing no one was about because they must appear a pair of drunks, unable to stay on their feet.

In the end, both of them fell in the same spot on the grass. First Thomas, then Evie on his lap.

'I cannot—' Thomas wheezed '—finish the race. If you feel inclined to go on, you win.'

The last thing she felt inclined to do was rise from his lap. Her victory was sitting where she was, seeing the joy that would have been natural to young Thomas transform grown-up Thomas.

Feeling him so close, leaning into the heat pulsing from him, she wondered if there might be hope for their marriage. Given time, would it become what she had always dreamed of?

Something shifted in his gaze. He looked at her the way a man looked at a woman he loved. But it could not be. She should not let her heart hope, at least not so quickly.

She tried to remind herself that the marriage she wanted was not the one he wanted. It was still love versus duty.

But he raised his hand to her hair, twined his fingers through the tresses, where they had fallen over her shoulders. Fascinated, she watched him draw the curls straight down towards her waist, then let them go so they looped across her bosom again.

'Do you agree that we are both winners?' he asked, his voice a low whisper.

'I was ahead at times but…I think perhaps you

caught up.' Did he understand she was not speaking of the race?

Full darkness settled around them, giving the feeling that there was no world but the one quietly closing them in.

'Shall we agree on a prize, one to be shared?' He stroked her cheek with the backs of his fingers.

'I will let you decide, Thomas.' She had enough to occupy her, trying to catch her breath, her heart.

'Good then…' He tipped her chin, lowered his lips. His breath, feeling so warm, smelling so male, puffed warmly against her face.

Distantly, she registered a sound on the path. Perhaps the squirrel they were not going to bring home.

'Thomas, there is something I want to tell you.' How could she keep her heart to herself any longer? When he kissed her this time she wanted him to know. 'I—'

'Even your brother did not shame us by kissing women in public.'

Oh, dear…no…this could not be real.

An older man who looked very much like Thomas stood a short distance away, arms crossed over his chest, glaring down at them.

As it was fully dark and the moon not yet risen, she could not see the Viscount's expression. Which was likely a good thing.

She could not see Thomas's expression either, but she felt it. She sensed he had been shot back to a time when, longing for his father's approval, he had been caught in boyish trouble. Perhaps to the moment when he had set aside childhood in favour of responsibility.

Please, oh, please, do not let him get stuck there. Do

not let him revert to the man who had no joy. She had only just restored him to who he had been.

'Welcome home, Father.'

'Welcome home to scandal at my front door, you mean.' He turned and walked along the path leading out of the park.

She and Thomas scrambled to their feet then hurried after him. She wished that her husband would speak to her, but he only strode beside her, not a word or a glance exchanged.

'Do not go back, Thomas,' she murmured.

'Where would we go if not home?' They were closer to the street now and she was able to see his expression in the glow of the lamps.

'I see you have already gone there, Thomas.'

'Where? What do you mean?' Still, he did not look at her but at his father's rigid steps, pressing towards Rivenhall.

'Away from me.'

'I am right here.'

But he wasn't here. Once again he was his father's heir, not the husband he had come so close to being.

Would she ever manage to get him back? She would weep were it not for the fact that she refused to be introduced to her father-in-law having tears on her face. He might mistake them for shame when really they were from heartache. And not for herself, but for her husband.

Who was Lord Rivenhall? He seemed an exceptionally stern fellow, walking ahead of them without so much as a word of greeting.

If he was anxious to meet his new daughter-in-law,

he hid it. If he felt joy in seeing his child after being away for so long, he hid it too.

She understood a great deal more about Thomas than she had moments ago. This man, this Viscount, striding through Rivenhall's gate ahead of them, was the one her husband had striven to be like since he was twelve years old.

No wonder Thomas had lost his joy with such an example to emulate.

However, Thomas's life was not the same as it had been when his father had gone to Scotland. Lord Rivenhall was not the only important influence in his son's life now.

Surely a wife held a great deal of influence.

Something in her began to stir—determination to not let her husband slip back into being the heir who shut his joy away in order to please someone else.

Now that she was over the shock of meeting Lord Rivenhall the way she had, although she had not actually met him, had she? But now that she had gathered her wits she intended to use them. Thomas's father was not the only one who loved him.

'My lord!' Evie hurried away from Thomas then climbed up the steps. Lord Rivenhall turned to look at her, his expression puzzled. 'In the surprise of meeting as we did... Well, the truth of it is, we did not actually meet—'

'I hope and pray that you are the lady who wed my son so suddenly.'

'Indeed, but who else would I be? I am not in the habit of sitting on strangers' laps in the park. And may I point out that you are greatly mistaken in thinking there is any scandal involved in the reason Thomas wed me. Well, at least on your son's part there is not.'

'But there was on your part?'

'I will let Thomas explain it to you. Rest assured your son is a hero and a man to be proud of. I certainly am.' She glanced over at Thomas, who had reached the top step and now stood beside them. This was not the moment to smile. But how could she not, seeing how father and son's brows dipped in the exact same way. It was simply endearing. 'Well, I am late dressing for dinner. It was lovely meeting you, my lord.'

She had her hand on the door knob when she heard, 'Welcome to Rivenhall, Evie.'

She would have felt better had he called her Mrs Grant. In her mind, using her marital title would mean he accepted her position in the household.

And yet, turning to nod at his greeting, she was stunned to see something in his eyes. It was the same expression Thomas had when he was withholding a smile. Having known him only a moment, she thought she must be wrong. Lord Rivenhall was clearly frowning.

'Thank you,' she answered anyway.

Chapter Sixteen

'Come to my study.'

Following his father, Thomas wondered if this was how William had felt on countless occasions when being brought to task for making a mistake. It had been a lifetime ago since Thomas had stood in shame before his father.

The Viscount sat down at his desk and sighed deeply. 'Sit down, Thomas.'

Not this time. William had always remained standing. He would do no less.

Never would he have imagined that he would be living up to his brother's example.

'Was there something disagreeable about Miss Brownton? I thought we agreed that she was our choice.'

'She was your choice, Father, not mine.' He only hoped that what he'd just said did not worsen his father's health. However, the truth was the truth and must be pointed out.

His father tilted his head and gave him a long look, but it did not seem to be the end of the world.

'But Miss Dumel was your choice?'

He could not say with all honesty that she had been... not at the time.

'There was more to it than that. It was my duty to offer to wed her.'

His father sagged. 'Please do sit down, son.'

Thomas slid into his customary chair. 'It is not what you are thinking. I did not compromise her...no one did.'

'I will admit you shook me for a moment, especially after what I witnessed in the park. But why then did you wed her? I am curious to know why she called you a hero.'

'I did what any man would. Evie was being kidnapped in front of Rivenhall.'

'Kidnapped! What in the blazes has been going on while I was away?'

He explained quickly what had happened.

'Marrying her keeps her out of their reach,' he finished.

'And out of your reach? She is very pretty and—'

'She is my wife. That is between us.'

His father arched a brow. He was not used to Thomas standing up to him. He wasn't used to it either.

Oddly it felt...liberating, made him sit taller in the chair.

'I do not mean to pry. It is only that under certain conditions an annulment can be had.'

Annulment? The possibility hit him like a blow. He had not even considered it.

He stood up, shaken to his soul.

His father might be thinking that with Evie out of the way he would be free to pursue Lydia.

Wedding Lydia had been the plan all along. If he put Evie aside in favour of the neighbour, his father would approve. Perhaps it would help whatever ailed him.

It was curious, though. His father appeared perfectly hale.

'How are you feeling, Father?'

'Feeling about what? You making such an important choice without me?'

'I was referring to your health.'

'My...? Oh, yes. Better. Northern air and all that. Quite restorative. Now, to the matter at hand.'

What matter at hand? 'Everything is in order, Father. The accounts are up to date.'

'The matter of dissolving your marriage.'

The statement cut him off at the knees. It was lucky he was already sitting.

He wanted his father's respect. It had always been most important to him. The question was, did he want it at the cost of giving up Evie?

Father or Evie—had it come to a choice? It felt that way.

The idea made him feel sick...lost.

He slid his chair back and stood up. 'I will see you at dinner, Father.'

Walking out of the study, he paused at the door to look back. He had the oddest sensation that his father had been smiling at him. If he had been, he was not now.

Surely he had imagined it.

'Do you know,' Thomas said, 'Lydia Brownton is the only one to have congratulated me on my marriage?'

'It goes to show how very suitable a lady she is.'

'It goes to show that she has no affection for me.'

'That matters very little for us.'

Something was wrong with this… He remembered how it used to be at Rivenhall.

'Didn't you love Mother?'

Now his father smiled. 'I adored her.'

Dinner that evening was uncomfortable. It was for Thomas at any rate. He imagined it could only be worse for his wife. His father's attitude upon meeting Evie for the first time had been offensive.

Now, here they sat, each with their own thoughts.

It might be better if there was at least a smattering of conversation.

His father shifted his attention from his meal to look steadily at Evie. Then he shifted it again to look even more steadily at him. Who knew what was going on in the Viscount's brain? Was he working out what to do with Evie once he got her dismissed from Rivenhall?

Why would he want to? Evie was acceptable in every way—as much a lady as any woman of society.

She was gracious, beautiful, fun—she made him laugh when he had thought he'd forgotten how to.

Clearly, laughter and fun were not a requirement in a bride as far as his father was concerned—as far as Thomas used to be concerned too. The puzzle of it was, his mother had been as bright as sunshine, always laughing and having fun. Had years of grief changed his father so much that he did not wish a happy marriage for his son?

Over the years Thomas had learned that duty fulfilled was happiness. It was what his father had taught him.

He looked at his wife. She set her fork aside, smiling at him. The occasional encouragement she sent his way made dinner a little more bearable.

Love was what mattered. That was what his wife had taught him.

Annulment? It could be done—but done by him?

To set a wife aside in such a heartless way was unthinkable. He could not believe the man he had looked up to all his life would actually consider it. His father was stern, but never cruel. Had he changed so greatly while he'd been in Scotland?

Or had Thomas been the one to change?

Earlier, Evie had wanted to tell him something—when he was leaning towards her for a kiss.

Lost in thought, he tapped his spoon on his plate, his eyes on his wife. The clink of silver on china echoed off the walls.

There had been intimacy between them, kisses only, but blistering ones. He wanted more. He wanted all of Evie. What was it she had been wanting to tell him in the park, when his father had come upon them?

If it was what he hoped, there would be no annulment. Even if it was not, there would be no annulment.

And why was his father smiling for no apparent reason?

Without warning, the dining room doors opened.

'I'm home!'

Minerva hurried across the room. Thomas was closest so he got the first hug. Seeing Evie, she gave a happy squeak and dashed for her. They hugged for a long time…until his father cleared his throat.

With a leap she launched herself at him and stood behind his chair, giving him hugs, kissing his cheek.

'I missed you so much, Father! Are you well? I am so glad you are home.'

His father never disguised his feelings for his only daughter, whether they be love or frustration. Sometimes both at the same time.

'Do I want to know what you have been up to while I was gone?'

'I doubt it. But we now have parrots.'

What an awful dinner! Until Minerva had arrived home from her visit to William's farm, the atmosphere had been dark, tense.

Thomas was troubled, she felt it to her bones. She knew he had spent time in his father's study, no doubt explaining their sudden marriage. She could only imagine it had not gone well.

The daughter-in-law Lord Rivenhall had long hoped for was not the one he'd got.

However, she was the one who loved Thomas…had been on the point of declaring it when they had been startled by the arrival of the Viscount.

Would it have made a difference if she'd had the chance to tell him?

As matters stood now, she was uncertain about what Thomas had in his heart for her. Had something shifted in his heart for her since their moments in the park?

But again, had being with his father, the man he respected and strove to be like, shifted it away again?

What had they discussed in the study?

It was crushing to think he belonged again only to Rivenhall. It was beyond frustrating that he did not return her smiles while they ate. Had her sister-in-law not arrived she might have run from the room weeping.

Now that everyone's attention was on news of Minerva's visit, she was going to leave the dining room. Except that she was not going to run and she was not going to weep.

But she did need time in her chamber. She might weep there. Something was not right with Thomas and she feared what it could mean.

She stood, making her excuses, and walked, her back stiffer than her heart. Halfway down the hallway she heard footsteps coming behind her. She turned.

Not Thomas. Her heart sagged further.

'One moment, Evie!'

She waited for him to catch up with her because she could not do what she wished to and run away from the formidable man.

'Yes, Lord Rivenhall.'

'I know that you must think me a cold man, uncaring of my son. But I know him. He has been preparing to be Viscount all his life. Nothing is more important to him than bringing honour to the title.'

'Yes, I know that.'

'Earlier, when we went to my study, we discussed what was to be done.'

'Done…about what, my lord?'

He did not answer, only looked thoughtfully at her.

'I believe you care for my son and want what is best for him.'

She did not need to say so—it had to be clear that she adored him. Lord Rivenhall had been there when she'd nearly told Thomas so.

'I will be honest—we did discuss an annulment.'

But of course they would have…and given they had come together as man and wife? Her mind was skittering so that she could hardly think. Her chest constricted so tightly she could not breathe either.

'I can see that you wish the best for him. I only ask that you give a great deal of thought to what that is.'

Apparently, that was all he had to say because he turned and walked back down the hallway.

Several feet away, he stopped and turned slowly to face her.

'I just want to say one more thing, my dear. I believe that this will all work out in your favour.'

That said, he headed back towards the dining room.

Annulment. It was only shock that kept her standing. Only crushing heartache that gave her legs what they needed to carry her to her chamber. The chamber with the door joining her room and Thomas's—the solidly locked door.

'You drove my wife from dinner.' Thomas stood when his father came back into the room. He needed to act, but was at a loss to know what to do.

'Did I? Perhaps it was you. As her husband I would think it falls to you to make sure she is comfortable at Rivenhall.'

But he had been… No, he had not. Hit with the truth, he could not recall anything he had done to put her at ease since they had married. He had closed himself in his study, buried his attention in his ledgers.

'It is time you made a choice. Is your loyalty to Rivenhall or to what you perceive as your duty to a stranger? I gave you a way out and only you can decide whether to take it or not.'

Minerva rounded on their father. 'What have you done? And Evie is not a stranger. She is my dearest friend in the world.'

'But is she your brother's? All I did was point out that there is yet time to seek an annulment...if that is his choice.'

'Oh...' His sister gave their father a small, sly-looking smile. 'Very clever. Well done, Father.'

'Clever? Minnie, he just acted like a miserable lout and drove Evie from the room. Next he will drive her from Rivenhall.'

'Do not be dense, Thomas. Our father has given you a choice. A chance to explore your heart and decide where to follow it.'

'He wishes for me to send my bride away so that I can court Lydia.'

'I never said that. I presented the possibility.' Their father and Minerva nodded at each other.

Why the blazes were they smiling? His life was in upheaval and they—

'It is because Father has given you a gift, Thomas.' How did his sister read him so easily? Evie did it to him too.

'A gift would have been him welcoming my wife to Rivenhall in a proper way.'

'One could point out that you have not done it.' Minerva came close, poking him in the chest with one finger. 'The gift is that Father has given you a choice.'

'Indeed, son. And just now I gave one to Evie. We shall see what happens.'

'You told her I wished to annul our marriage?' He felt blown over.

'I merely asked her to look within her heart. Determine what was best for you.'

'You did not need to test Evie that way, Father. I know she loves Thomas.'

'But I have only just met her. I only hope she makes the right choice.'

'I only hope that Thomas does. What will it be, brother? Your wife or Rivenhall?'

He shook his head. 'I cannot believe the two of you.'

With that, he left them.

Running towards the stairs, his heart swelled with an ache that nearly brought him to his knees. Dark shame swallowed him whole. It had taken his father's manipulation to make him see the truth.

He loved his wife, desperately and with every bit of his soul. And he knew she loved him. It was what she had been about to tell him in the park. He had no doubt of it now.

She loved him so much that he feared she would leave him. That she would think he wanted to put Rivenhall before her. There was no reason to think she would not, since he had never given her any reason to believe he did not put it first.

He dashed up the stairs, taking them two at a time.

* * *

What Evie wanted to do was seduce her husband. That was the only way she knew of to make sure he could not put her aside. Dismiss her as if she was nothing to him at all.

The problem with that idea was that she did not know the first thing about seducing a man. Hips were enticing to males. She had read it somewhere. If she knew how to make them sway as she walked, and if she put on a sheer nightgown while she sashayed about the chamber, it might help.

But no…in order for her to seduce Thomas she would need for the door to somehow open, not remain steadfastly locked against her feminine wiles. Such as they were.

But of course she was not going to do it, even if the door did miraculously open. Seduction was akin to deception. She would not deceive Thomas again. It was not how love behaved. Love wanted what was best for the other person.

Lord Rivenhall had been correct in suggesting she think hard about what was best for him.

Her new husband was dedicated to Rivenhall, showed his devotion to it in everything he did and in everything he had done since he was a boy.

He had even been willing to enter a loveless marriage for the sake of the place he loved.

He had been willing to marry her, too, but because she was in danger and he was honourable.

Well, then…thinking did not take nearly as long as she'd thought it would. Truth shouted rather loudly in her face; it took her heart and squeezed until she imagined her chest filling with blood...and tears.

Grief hit her so deeply she nearly went down on her knees. Once again she was going to run away from this place she loved. She'd thought for a short time she belonged here, but no—Thomas belonged here with his society bride.

Perhaps he would be happy with her one day.

But Evie...she would never be happy again.

Going to her wardrobe, she drew out her clothes, only the ones she could carry away quickly. She must be away from here before Thomas knew she was gone.

It was unlikely that he would come after her this time. Even Minerva would not send him in this instance.

Finished shoving who knew what into her valise, she swiped her arm across her eyes.

She must love her husband...but no, he had never actually been that if an annulment could be had, but Thomas, she must love him very much to be walking away when her heart was screaming at her not to.

Again, that was not how love behaved.

'Come, Charm.' She scooped the kitten off the bed. 'We must go.'

Rushing into his chamber, Thomas searched the dresser drawer. Where the blazes was the blasted key to the door between their rooms? If he did not find it in two seconds he would knock on the hallway door to his wife's chamber. He would rather not alert the household to what was going on, but he would if he had to.

Ah! There the rascal was. He clutched the cold brass

in his fist, rushed to the door and turned the key in the lock.

The door squealed when it opened.

What was this?

'Evie?' She stood in the doorway, one foot in the chamber and the other in the hall. She clutched her valise in one hand, held Charm close to her chest with the other. 'What are you doing?'

'You opened the door.' She hiccupped, sniffed.

'Are you leaving?'

'I must.'

The key fell out of his fingers. He heard it tinkle on the floor while he strode towards his wife. He took the valise from her fingers and set it near the wall.

'Why? If it was because of my father... Evie, please do not go.'

'I must, Thomas. You know it is right.'

'I do not know it and I do not know why you think so.'

He took the kitten from her and set it on the floor.

'Well, I could not seduce you because I do not know how and it would also be deceitful... I will not deceive you again. Nor will I hold you to me that way.'

'My father told me what he said to you. I am truly sorry.'

'Oh, but, Thomas, he was right to say it. It is your way out of this marriage. I understand that you only did it to protect me.'

She looked so small, so very sad and defeated standing there. He ought to have recognised his feelings for her long ago. What a dunce he was, confusing friendship and love.

'Will you sit with me for a moment? Help me understand why you wish to leave Rivenhall.' That wasn't really what he meant to say, not what was in his heart. He was not pleading for Rivenhall, he was pleading for himself. 'Why you wish to leave me.'

'I do not wish to. But I love you far too much to stand in the way of what you want.'

'Are you certain you know what I want?'

'You have made it rather clear, Thomas. Truly, you would not be stuck in a marriage you did not plan for had I not run away. I would never have become Minerva's companion and then my relative would not have come here looking for me and you ending up forced to wed me. Forced by honour, but still, it is what you did.'

'Made a great muddle of things is what I did.'

Standing, she sniffed again, bit her lip and blinked damp, red eyes.

'Well, the sooner I am on my way, the sooner you can work out the muddle with Lydia. Although—' he noticed her fingers trembling '—it will be difficult. You might need to ask Minerva for advice... And... Well... goodbye, Thomas.'

He rose, following her as she backed towards the door.

'It is not Lydia I must work things out with. It is you, love.'

She blinked, probably taken aback by the endearment.

'I shall send you my address when I settle. You may write to me.'

'Is there a pen and paper in that drawer?' He nodded towards the writing desk.

'Yes, but what…'

'I am writing to you now. Will you wait? Please, Evie, do not leave until you read what I have to say.'

'Very well.' She returned to the bed and sat down.

He wrote quickly, revealing his heart as best he could with a pen. After she read it he would use his mouth to tell her. Then, if she believed him, if she wanted him, he would show her again, with his mouth.

He came back to the bed, sat down next to her and handed her the letter.

'Will you read it to me?' she asked.

'First I shall kiss you.' He did, but quickly since things were not yet settled between them.

'I love you, Violet Evie Dumel Grant. I was an idiot not to recognise it the first time I saw you with pollen on your nose. You are all that is bright and happy in my life. Please, do not go away.'

He gave her the letter. She pressed it to her heart.

'Truly, Thomas?'

'Ah, Evie, it is the truest thing I have ever written. I love you. I do not want any other wife but you. If you go away I will never marry again.'

'But, Thomas, what about—'

He pressed his fingers to her lips.

'You were right all along. I see it now. There is only one reason to marry and that is for love. It is why I married you. It wasn't to protect you, as I claimed it was. I could have sent you to America or India, where you would have been safe. But I wanted you. I was just too dense to know it was because I loved you.'

She was silent for a long time, weighing his future probably. He had meant it when he said he would not wed if she left him. If she was not Viscountess, no one would be. Then she leaned sideways, resting her head on his shoulder.

'It would appear I packed my valise for no reason.'

'Does that mean you will stay? Our marriage will not be annulled?'

Lifting her head, she touched his cheek, traced a line down his face with her finger as if she were following the track of a tear.

He did not know he had been crying, but perhaps it happened just now, because of relief, of utter and complete joy.

'It will not be annulled. I will stay and love you every day of my life.'

'I intend to love you every day of my life, too, Mrs Grant.' He kissed her, slowly lowering her back on the bed. 'And every night...beginning with this one...with this minute. I do not intend to let you change your mind in the morning. You are mine, Evie. Mine to love and cherish, starting right now.'

'Carry on, Mr Grant. I do not intend to let you change your mind either.'

Hours later, love for her broke as bright as sunrise in his heart. It sparkled as a precious diamond on a wedding band, burned hot as the mattress of the marriage bed.

In her sleep, she nestled her cheek against his shoulder, draped her arms across his chest. Her riot of curls tickled his nose.

He could scarcely believe what he'd come so close to missing out on.

'In spite of it all,' he murmured, 'we have found our love match.'

She smiled in her sleep so he thought she'd heard him, but he would tell her again when she awoke.

Perhaps he would tell her every morning for the rest of their lives.

It was late afternoon the next day when Mr and Mrs Grant re-joined life—a life which was, in Evie's opinion, amazingly grand. How could it not be when something had happened which she'd once feared unlikely to happen? Thomas now shared the belief that love and marriage went together...there was no point to it otherwise. As unlikely as it had once seemed, she had made her love match.

She clung to her husband's elbow while he hugged one arm around her shoulders as they walked towards his father's study. Thomas had told her he needed to make it clear to his father that there would be no annulment...in case he did not already suspect it. In case it had not been his father's purpose all along to force his son into choosing what he wished for his life, not what duty expected of him.

It took a great deal of time to walk the distance of the hallway because it seemed they could not take twenty steps without stopping for a kiss, for a declaration of love.

'Ah, there you are!'

Apparently, they would not need to go all the way to the study to find her father-in-law. He stepped out of the small drawing room with a great grin.

My stars, he and his son were alike in what a smile

could do to transform their expressions. Now she understood who her husband had inherited his handsome face from.

'Children, walk with me in the garden.'

They were not all the way down the garden steps before Thomas informed his father there would be no annulment. On the off-chance he'd thought so, it was now spoken and confirmed.

'My dear!' Lord Rivenhall stepped forward, took both of her hands in his and squeezed them. 'I cannot say how pleased I am that my son came to his senses. Welcome to Rivenhall, Mrs Grant.'

She was not going to weep again, but her throat did swell hearing her father-in-law call her that.

'Thank you...'

'Father—I hope you will call me that. And I apologise for our first meeting. I was tired from travel and there had been rumours.'

'I quite understand. It must have looked like—'

'A young couple in love,' he said. 'I ought to have recognised it right off. That whole thing about the annulment was only my heavy-handed way of making sure my son understood his own heart. Thomas is very dear to me, you understand.'

She did understand. 'He is to me as well, exceptionally dear.'

Standing as close as they were, she felt Thomas take a quick breath. Naturally it would mean a great deal to him to hear this spoken aloud by his father.

Not as much by her, since she had told him that last night no less than...it was countless times.

'My wife was exceptionally dear to me too. I see Thomas in her.'

'You do? I thought William was the one just like her.'

'He is, of course. He looks like her and acts like her. She was a lively lady and…and quite wonderful. But, Thomas, there was more to her than that. I suppose you were too young understand. To you she was simply Mother, but she was the most loving and loyal of women—in that you remind me of her.'

Thomas turned about as if looking at something that had caught his attention in the garden. No doubt he was fighting not to weep, to be manly and lordly.

'Father, there is something I must know. Please tell me the truth. I promise I shall bear up under the news.'

'What is it, son? It sounds rather dire.'

'How are you feeling? Are you as recovered as you seem to be?'

'Ah, yes…about that. I was not as ill as I made it seem. A small cold is all it was.'

'But I thought—'

'As you were intended to think, my boy. I only wanted you to find your own wings, so to speak. I must say you did a grand job of it. I am more proud of you than you will ever know.'

How wonderful for Thomas to hear that. It was what he had longed for all his life and now she wanted to weep, in case she had not done enough of it last night.

'Come along, my dears.' Minerva's voice carried through the garden.

She had been away from home for several hours, not that Evie and Thomas had paid much attention to her absence because they had been quite involved in important matters. Matters they would engage in again as soon as they had something to eat.

'What on God's good earth are those?' her father-in-law exclaimed.

Evie clapped a hand over her mouth. She felt Thomas stifle a gasp.

'Why, Father, they are dogs, of course.'

'But why are they pink?'

Thomas took Evie's elbow and quickly led her away. At the terrace steps he glanced over his shoulder.

'Welcome home, Father.'

Summer 1889

Thomas thought the family ought to return to the house before rain began to fall. The conservatory was snug enough, but it would be a wet walk back to the house.

While it was good to see William and Elizabeth's children dashing about in a game of chase pursued by their grandfather, Thomas had it in mind to get his wife alone in their suite of rooms, or as alone as was possible these days.

'Are you still competing with your brother?' Evie asked, sitting on the bench beside him and smiling down at their twin daughters, one resting in her arms and one nestled in his. 'It seems to me that you are.'

'It is only a rare coincidence that we both are the father of twins.'

His brother, coming out of the aviary, spotted them then walked over to coo at the babies.

They smiled at their uncle. Happy little dimples in

their round, pink cheeks proved that his brother was still a charmer. Only the ladies he was charming now were only four months old.

'I shall wait a year and then see what I can do about catching up with you, William.' Thomas glanced at the bench near the aviary.

'I look forward to it, as long as my sister-in-law is agreeable.'

William went back to where Elizabeth sat upon a bench. She pressed her hand into the small of her back and stretched.

'I knew it, you still want to compete with your brother.'

'Both of us knew those were simply playful words. Do not worry, love. We will have these dashing about before we consider welcoming another child.'

'In my heart I am ready now. But yes, we shall wait.'

'William says this birth ought to be easier on Elizabeth. She assures him it is only one baby.'

'From the look of things, it will be born right here at Rivenhall.' Judging by Evie's smile, nothing would make her happier.

'Evie Grant, may I tell you again how much I adore you?'

'Oh, yes, Thomas, do carry on.'

'But I mean it. Every time I tell you I mean it more.' He lifted his child higher in his arms, kissed her plump cheek, then buried his nose in the downy fluff of her hair. There truly was nothing like the smell of a baby. 'I wonder, do you think Minerva will ever find her senses and wed?'

'I do not believe she has misplaced them.'

'But she has. My sister needs to marry, and not for the reason I used to believe. I only think, in spite of what she says, she would be happy as a married lady.'

'Perhaps, Thomas, but she is the one who needs to think so.'

'I only wish for her to have the happiness we have.'

'I pray every day for her to find it.'

'Yes, well…knowing my sister, I suppose nothing but Divine intervention will do.'

His babies cooed, both of them at the same time. They were the delight of a lifetime. His heart swelled with gratitude at how he had been blessed.

'Father!' William called.

Lord Rivenhall paused in the pursuit of his grandchildren. 'Make it quick—I am falling behind.'

'You will wear the children out,' William answered. 'They will never settle if you keep them so wound up.'

Thomas scarcely recognised his formerly irresponsible brother. He gave Elizabeth the credit, naturally.

Love, he now believed, changed everything.

'Who is that man?' Thomas called across the conservatory at his brother, who had taken over rubbing his wife's back.

'I am who I always have been—Father's favourite,' William called back, grinning.

'Father!' Thomas waved to get his father's attention. 'Who is your favourite child?'

'Minerva!' Their father grinned, then continued the pursuit of his grandchildren.

'I knew it!' His sister's voice came from the entrance of the conservatory. 'The two of you have been trying to outdo each other all these years when all along it was me.'

'You are our favourite, Thomas.' Evie leaned sideways to kiss his cheek.

Well, then, being the favourite of his wife and daughters would always be more than enough for him.

'That, my dear wife, is the highest praise I could hope for.'

Her words, so warmly brushing his ear, reminded him that he wanted to retire upstairs.

'Where have you been all day, Minnie?' Thomas asked.

'I was up to something rather important.'

'That sounds intriguing. What were you doing?' Thomas was half-afraid to know. His sister had been away from home more often lately. Spending time with friends was what she said. But with friends…doing what? That was the real question.

'Something of great value.' She glanced at their father and took a deep breath with her hands folded in front of her.

'You know her better than anyone, Evie,' Thomas whispered. 'What do you think it is?'

'I think your father hopes she will announce that she wishes to begin courting that young man who has been coming around.'

'Which one? There are several Father has been encouraging her to give her attention to.'

Evie shook her head. The scent of lavender wafted over the inches separating them. The fragrance never failed to make his heart beat a little harder and the blood thrum through his veins a little hotter. It was time to rise from the bench, to take his family upstairs to their suite of rooms, put the babies down for a nap and...

'It isn't that...but I cannot imagine what it is,' Evie murmured.

'I wonder if she has brought home an orphaned gaggle of ducks or a wandering piglet.'

'No...it has been some time since she brought home a stray animal.'

'Come upstairs with me now, Evie. Whatever it is we can discover it later. Being this close to you is making me mad to get you alone.' He glanced at the child in his arms and shrugged. 'Or as alone as family bliss will allow.'

Evie gave a quiet laugh, soft and seductive. She had refused to hire a nurse to care for the children, wanting to care for them herself, so they would manage what seduction could be had. Which was fine. He would not change a thing about his life.

'All right, but let's leave slowly,' she whispered. 'I have never seen your sister appear apprehensive before. I am on pins to know what valuable thing she has been doing.'

'What important thing?' Their father paused in his game of chase to ask.

Standing, Thomas nodded to Evie and sent her a silent message that this was their chance to slip away.

She smiled at the promise he delivered with one glance. He could not have imagined how much he would enjoy marriage. Having someone in the world with whom he could carry on a conversation without words was beyond price. An intimacy beyond compare.

He slipped one hand around Evie's waist when she

rose, hugging the baby he carried closer. Arching a brow at his wife, he told her that he agreed this moment was growing quite interesting and they ought to hurry away...slowly.

'Minerva, my dear.' Her father hurried over to her and cupped her shoulders with his hands and peered closely at her face. 'Tell me a young man has caught your attention.'

'Have you found a new cause, perhaps?' William asked with both a grin and a frown.

'Well, no.' She glanced quickly at Thomas, then back at their father. 'It is much better than that.'

'Indeed, a young man is not a cause, precisely.' Their father's voice sounded hopeful.

'I do not have a cause so much as an occupation. I have taken employment...at London Cradle. You know it—the orphanage.'

No one spoke because... The daughter of a Viscount? Working for a wage?

Heaven help them all.

Especially their father.

* * * * *

*If you enjoyed this story, be sure to check out the first
book in The Rivenhall Weddings miniseries*

Inherited as the Gentleman's Bride

And look out for more in the series, coming soon!

*Whilst you're waiting, why not check out
Carol Arens's other great reads?*

The Viscount's Christmas Proposal
'A Kiss Under the Mistletoe' *in*
A Victorian Family Christmas
To Wed a Wallflower
The Viscount's Yuletide Bride